LOVE IN ANOTHER TOWN

Barbara Taylor Bradford was born in Leeds, and was a reporter for the *Yorkshire Evening Post* at sixteen. By the age of twenty she had graduated to London's Fleet Street as both editor and columnist. In 1979 she wrote her first novel, *A Woman of Substance*, and that enduring bestseller was followed by twelve others: *Voice of the Heart, Hold the Dream, Act of Will, To Be the Best, The Women in his Life, Remember, Angel, Everything to Gain, Dangerous to Know, Love in Another Town, Her Own Rules* and *A Secret Affair*. Seven have been made into television mini-series and three more are currently in production. Her novels have sold more than 55 million copies worldwide in more than 88 countries and 38 languages. Mrs Bradford lives in New York City and Connecticut with her husband, film producer Robert Bradford.

BARBARA TAYLOR BRADFORD

Love in Another Town

HarperCollins*Publishers*

HarperCollins*Publishers*
77–85 Fulham Palace Road,
Hammersmith, London W6 8JB

Special overseas edition 1996
This paperback edition 1996
3 5 7 9 8 6 4

First published in Great Britain by
HarperCollins*Publishers* 1995

ISBN 0 00 649822 1

Set in Palatino by
Rowland Phototypesetting Ltd,
Bury St Edmunds, Suffolk

Printed and bound in Great Britain by
Caledonian International Book Manufacturing Ltd, Glasgow

For my dearest husband Bob,
to whom I owe so much

CHAPTER
1

JAKE CANTRELL SLOWED his pick-up truck as he approached Lake Waramaug near the Boulders Inn, came to a standstill and gazed out of the window.

The lake was still; it held a glassy sheen, looked almost silver in the late afternoon light of this cool April day. He lifted his eyes to the etiolated sky, so bleached out that it, too, seemed as pale and as unmoving as the water. In stark contrast were the rolling hills rising up around the lake, darkly green and lush with trees.

Jake could not help thinking once again how beautiful the view was from this angle: a dreamy landscape of water and sky. To Jake, it was somehow evocative, reminded him of another place, yet he was not sure of where ... some place somewhere he had never been, except in his imagination perhaps . . . England, France, Italy or Germany, maybe even Africa. Some place he would like to go one day. If he ever got the chance. He had always wanted to travel, dreamed about going to exotic lands, but thus far in his twenty-eight years of life on this planet he had only been to New York City a few times, and twice to Atlanta where his sister Patty was now living.

Shading his eyes with one hand, Jake scanned the vistas of land, water and sky once more, then nodded. How incredible the light is today, almost otherworldly, he thought, as he stared ahead.

He had always been fascinated by light, both natural and artificial. The latter he worked with on a daily basis, the former he frequently endeavoured to capture on canvas, when he had time to pick up a paintbrush and indulge himself. He loved to paint whenever he could, even though he wasn't very good at it. But it gave him a great sense of satisfaction, just as did creating special lighting effects. He was working on a big lighting job now, one that was tough, tested his talent and imagination and fired his creativity. He loved the challenge.

The car behind him honked him forward, and, rousing himself from his thoughts, he pushed his foot down on the accelerator and drove on.

Jake headed along Route 45 North which would take him up to Route 341 and all the way to Kent. As he drove he kept noticing the unusual clarity of the light today; it echoed the light over the lake and seemed to get even brighter the farther north he drove.

Lately he had come to realize that this clear bright light was endemic to this part of the state, called the northwestern highlands by some, the Litchfield Hills by others. He did not care what people called the area. All he knew was that it was beautiful, so breathtaking he thought of it as God's own country. And the extraordinary, incandescent skies, almost uncanny at times, inspired awe in him.

This particular area was relatively new to him, even though he had been born in Hartford, had grown up there, and had lived in Connecticut all his life. For the past four-and-a-half years he had been a resident of New Milford, but he had rarely ventured beyond the town's boundaries. That is until a year ago, just after he had finally separated from his wife Amy.

He had stayed on in New Milford, living alone in a small studio on Bank Street for almost a year. It was around then that he had started driving into the countryside, going farther afield, looking for a new place to live, something a bit better than the studio, an apartment or, preferably, a small house.

It was on Route 341 near Kent that he had found the little white clapboard three months ago. It had taken him a few weeks to get it cleaned up, painted and made reasonably habitable, then he had scoured the local junk shops and sales looking for furniture. He was surprised at the things he managed to find, at prices which he considered reasonable. In no time at all he had managed to make the little clapboard fresh-looking and comfortable. His final purchases were a brand new bed, a good rug and a television set, all bought in one of the big stores in Danbury.

Finally, he had moved in three weeks ago and had felt like a king in his castle ever since.

Jake drove on at a steady speed, not thinking about anything in particular except getting home. *Home.* He found himself contemplating that word all of a sudden.

It hovered there in his mind. 'Home,' he said out loud. And yes, he *was* going home. Home to his house. He savoured this thought, liking it. A smile lingered on his sensitive mouth. *Home. Home. Home.* The word suddenly had a very special meaning to him. It signified so much.

It struck him then that never in nine years of marriage to Amy had he ever called their various apartments home; usually, whenever he referred to them, he would say *our place*, or *back at the ranch*, or some such thing.

Now he realized that until today the word *home* had always meant the house in Hartford where he had been raised by his parents, John and Annie Cantrell, both dead for several years.

But the little white clapboard on Route 341, with its picket fence and neat garden, was indeed home, and it had become his haven, his place of refuge. There were several adjoining fields with a large barn standing in one of them, and this he had turned into a workshop and studio. Currently, he was renting the property, but he liked it so much he was seriously thinking of buying it. *If* he could get a mortgage from the bank in New Milford. *If* the owner would sell. Jake wasn't sure about either possibility at this moment. He could only hope.

Apart from being the right size, the house was close enough to Northville, where he had moved his electrical business a few weeks ago. He had wanted to be out of New Milford altogether because Amy still lived and worked there. Not that there was any animosity between them; in fact, they were quite good friends in spite of their break-up.

Their separation had been reasonably amicable, although initially she had not wanted to let him go. Eventually she had agreed. What option did she have? He had been long gone from her emotionally and physically, even when they still shared the same apartment in New Milford. The day he had finally packed his bags and made his intentions clear for the last time, she had exclaimed, 'Okay, Jake, I agree to a separation. But let's stay friends. *Please.*'

Long absent in spirit, and with one foot already out of the door, he had willingly agreed. What harm could it do? And, anyway, if it mollified her so much the better. Anything to make his escape easier, to get away from her at long last, in a peaceful way and without another row.

Jake's thoughts centred entirely on Amy for a moment or two. In many ways he felt sorry for her. She wasn't a bad person. Just dull, unimaginative and something of a killjoy. Over the years she had become an albatross around his neck, dragging him down, and inducing in him an unfamiliar state of depression.

He knew that he was bright and quick and clever. He always had been, even as a child. And he was good at his job. His former boss at Bolton Electric had constantly told him he was a genius with lighting and special effects. And because of his drive, hard work and talent he had moved up in life; he had wanted to move even farther, but she had held him back.

Amy was always afraid – afraid things would go wrong if they did anything out of the ordinary, or if he made a move to better himself and them and their existence. She had fought him two years ago when he had left Bolton Electric and started his own business.

'It's not going to work, it'll fail and then where will we be?' she had wailed. 'Anyway, what do you know about being a contractor?' she had gone on nervously, her face pinched and white and tight-lipped. When he hadn't answered her, she had added, 'You're a good electrician, Jake, I know that. But you're not good at business.'

He had been infuriated by her remark. Glaring at her, he had shot back, 'How do you know what I'm good at? You haven't been interested in me or anything I do for years.'

She had gaped at him, obviously shocked, but he was speaking the truth. It seemed to him now, as he remembered those words, that Amy had lost interest in him during the second year of their marriage.

Jake sighed. It had all become so sad and discouraging, and he wondered, for the umpteenth time, how it could have gone so wrong. They had grown up together in Hartford, had been childhood sweethearts, and had married right out of school. Well, almost. In those days the future had glittered brightly for him, had been full of promise.

He had his dreams and ambitions. Unfortunately Amy had neither. Within a few years he had come to realize that she not only fought change with great tenacity but actually feared it.

Whatever he wanted to do to grow, to make things better for them, she threw cold water on it. Five years into the marriage he had begun to feel that he was drowning in all that cold water of hers.

The future with Amy had started to look so bleak, so without promise or happiness, that he had eventually begun to drift away from her.

Content to plod along, following her usual routine, she had never even noticed when he was gone from her in body and spirit. He might live in the same apartment but he was no longer really there.

Inevitably, he strayed and had a couple of affairs with other women and discovered he didn't even feel guilty. He had also realized at the time – over two years ago now – that the game was up between them. Jake was not a promiscuous man, and the very act of infidelity told him that there was nothing left of their relationship, nothing left to salvage. At least for him.

Through her apathy and fear, her lack of trust in him and in his ability, Amy had killed their marriage. She had taken hope away from him.

Everyone needed hope ... everyone needed dreams. What did a man have, for God's sake, if not his dreams? Amy had trampled on his.

And yet he did not blame her; he felt sorry for her, perhaps because he had known her for so long, nearly all of his life. Then again, he was aware that she had never meant to hurt him in any way. Amy gave so little of herself she therefore had so little. She was missing out on life.

Amy was still pretty in a pale blonde way, but she did nothing to help her delicate colouring, so she appeared faded and drab these days. And she had put on weight. Not a lot, only a few pounds, but because she was small that bit of extra weight made her look dumpy.

She'll never get married again, Jake thought with a sudden flash of insight, and groaned inwardly. He would probably end up paying her alimony forever, until the day she died. Or he did. But what the hell, he didn't care. He knew he could always make money. He had an unfailing self-confidence.

Jake slowed the pick-up when he came to his white clapboard house, pulled into the yard and parked in front of the garage. Walking around to the back, he let himself into the kitchen.

Home, he thought, and glanced around the room. Then he grinned. He *was* home. He *was* free. He had his own business now, and it was doing well. He had a bright future again. His dreams were intact after all. Nobody could take them away. He was at peace with himself. And with the world at large. He was even at peace with Amy, in his own way. Eventually they would divorce and truly go their separate ways.

And if he was lucky he would meet another woman one day and fall in love. He would get married again. And hopefully there would be a child. Maybe even children. A wife, a home, a family, and his own business. Those were the things he wanted and it seemed to him that they were simple, fundamental things. Certainly there was nothing complicated about them. Yet Amy had made them seem unattainable because she had not wanted them. She hadn't even wanted to have a child. She'd been afraid of that too.

'What if there's something wrong with the baby?' she had said to him once, just after he had told her he wanted to have a child. 'What if the baby's born defective in some way? What would we do, Jake? I wouldn't want a defective baby.'

Startled, he had stared at her in complete bafflement, frowning, not understanding how she could mouth such things. It was then that he had felt a spurt of anger inside, and that anger had stayed with him for a very long time.

Just over a year ago he had realized that Amy had cheated him of life for the entire time they had been married. To him that was a crime. But then he had allowed her to do it, hadn't he? You were only a victim if you permitted yourself to be one, his mother had told him once. He reminded himself not to forget that.

Amy was so negative she was a genuine loser. He had tried to help her to change but she had looked at him blankly, obviously not understanding what he was getting at.

Suddenly impatient with himself, he pushed away thoughts of Amy. After all, she was on her own now. As was he.

Opening the fridge door, Jake took out a beer, prised off the cap with the opener on the counter, then stood leaning against the sink, drinking from the bottle, enjoying it; beer always tasted better from the bottle.

The phone began to ring. He reached for it. 'Hello?'

'Jake, is that you?'

He straightened slightly on hearing the voice. 'Yes, it is. How're you, Samantha?'

'I'm fine, Jake, thanks. You haven't forgotten the meeting tonight, have you?'

'No, I haven't. But I'm running late. Just got in from work. I'll be there soon. Real soon.'

'Don't kill yourself. I'm late myself today. I'll see you at the theatre.'

'Okay.' He glanced at the kitchen clock. It was just turning five-thirty. 'In about an hour?'

'That's good for me. 'Bye.'

'See you later,' Jake said, and hung up.

He finished the beer and went through into the bedroom. After pulling off his boots and jeans he stripped off his heavy sweater, T-shirt and underpants, then strode into the bathroom to take a shower.

Five minutes later he was towelling himself dry, and after putting on a terry-cloth robe he padded through into the small living room.

Standing in front of his CD player, his eyes scanned the shelf of discs next to it. He had inherited his love of music from his mother, especially classical music and opera. She had had a beautiful voice, and he had been reared on Verdi and Puccini, as well as Mozart, Rachmaninoff, Tchaikovsky, and other great composers. He'd always thought it a pity his mother had not been able to have the proper musical education and training, since in his opinion she'd had a voice worthy of the Metropolitan Opera in New York City.

Automatically, his hand reached for one of her favourites, Puccini's *Tosca*, but after looking at the Maria Callas disc for a moment he put it back, pulled out another one, a selection of Puccini and Verdi arias sung by Kiri Te Kanawa, whose voice he loved and who was his preferred opera star. After turning the volume up, he went back to the bathroom, leaving all of the doors open so that he could enjoy the music.

Staring at himself in the bathroom mirror, Jake ran a hand over his chin. No two ways about it, he needed a shave. He lathered himself with soap and scraped the razor over his chin, rinsed his face, combed back his damp black hair and then went back into the bedroom, all the while listening to Te Kanawa singing arias from *Don Carlos*, *Il Trovatore*, and *La Traviata*.

By the time he was dressed in clean blue jeans, a fresh blue-and-white checked shirt and a dark blue sports jacket, she was still singing.

One of the arias he liked the most was 'Vissi d'arte' from *Tosca*, and now he walked through into the living room, touched the track number for *Tosca* on the CD player and sat down. He didn't want to be late for the meeting with Samantha Matthews, but he did want to hear his favourite piece from *Tosca*.

As Te Kanawa's voice filled the room, soared up to the rafters, Jake was engulfed. He felt himself falling down into her wonderful voice, falling into the music, which never failed to touch him with its beauty and sadness.

Te Kanawa *was* Tosca, and she was singing of her

19

sorrow, her tribulation, her hour of need, and Jake leaned his head back against the chair, closed his eyes, gave himself up to the music.

Unexpectedly, he felt choked. Tears welled. His emotions were suddenly laid bare . . . he was filled with yearning . . . for something . . . although he was not exactly sure what he yearned for. Then he knew . . . he wanted to *feel* again. I know there's more, he thought, there's got to be more to life . . .

He let the music wash over him, relaxing his body, and he remained very still even after the aria had finished. In repose, his lean, sharply-sculpted face looked much less troubled.

After a short while Jake roused himself, and went to turn off the CD player. He had to be in Kent in five minutes, and it would take him longer than that to get there.

He left the house through the kitchen, and ran to his pick-up truck.

On the way to Kent he thought about the meeting he was about to have with Samantha Matthews. He had met her a few weeks ago on the big lighting job he was doing at a mansion in nearby Washington. She was a resident of the town who designed and produced unusual, handmade fabrics which the owner, his current client, was using throughout the house.

He and Samantha had started talking over a cup of coffee one day, when they were at the house together, and she had been interested in hearing more about the special lighting effects he was creating inside the house and in the grounds.

Several days later she had phoned him with an offer. It was an invitation to work with her on the stage sets for an amateur dramatic group she was involved with in Kent.

He had agreed to come to one meeting at least. And it was tonight. He had no idea what to expect, and he wasn't sure whether it would be the first and last, or the first of many.

Although he had not told Samantha, he was excited about working in the theatre, if only with an amateur group such as hers. It was a wonderful challenge and a way to learn more, he felt.

As he drove towards Kent, his mind preoccupied with lighting techniques, Jake Cantrell had no idea that he was being propelled towards his destiny. Nor did he have any way of knowing that his life was about to change, and so profoundly it would never be the same again.

Later, when he looked back to this night, he would do so wonderingly, reminding himself how ordinary it had seemed. He would ask himself why he had not sensed that something momentous was going to happen, why he had not realized that he was about to set out on the journey of his life.

CHAPTER
2

SAMANTHA MATTHEWS LOOKED UP from the script she was making notations on and stared across the table at her friend Maggie Sorrell, frowning. 'Now you tell me you think I've chosen the wrong play! Just when I've got it cast and everyone's madly learning their lines!' she exclaimed, her voice rising slightly.

'I didn't say that!' Maggie protested. 'I asked you why you'd chosen it. I was merely thinking out loud. Honestly.'

'Thinking out loud or not, you sounded critical.'

'I didn't, Sam!'

'Doubtful, then.'

'Not doubtful either. You know very well I never doubt you, or anything you do. I really was only wondering why this particular play, that's all.'

Samantha nodded. 'Okay, I believe you. I know you're my true blue friend who's stuck by me through thick and thick and thin and thin over the years. My very best friend in the world.'

'Just as you're mine,' Maggie murmured. 'So come on, tell me. Why did you pick *The Crucible?*'

'Because last year, before you'd come to live here, we did *Annie Get Your Gun*, and I didn't want to direct a musical again. I wanted to stage a drama. Preferably one by a great American playwright who was still alive; that's why I chose an Arthur Miller play. But I must admit, there's also another reason –'

'Because we did it at Bennington all those years ago,' Maggie cut in knowingly, smiling. 'That's it, isn't it?'

Samantha sat back in her chair and regarded her friend intently for a moment, then she shook her head slowly. 'No, not at all.'

'And I thought you'd chosen it for sentimental reasons.' Maggie made a face and shrugged. 'Oh silly me.'

'Sentimental reasons?' Samantha echoed.

'Of course. We were nineteen and rapidly becoming fast friends. Best friends, actually. We'd both fallen in love for the first time; also, we were treading the boards for the first time. In *The Crucible*. It was a very special year for us, but you'd forgotten, hadn't you?'

'No, I do remember that year at college. It was 1971. In fact, I thought about it only the other day. And in a way you're correct. When I selected *The Crucible* I *was* playing it a bit safe, because I do know it so well.

But when I said I chose it for another reason it was because Arthur Miller lives in Connecticut and we're a Connecticut theatrical group. So, call me sentimental if you like, Mag.'

'You are a sentimentalist at heart, even though you like to pretend you're not,' Maggie answered.

'Maybe I am,' Samantha agreed and laughed. 'Although there are those who call me bossy.'

'Oh you're that all right!' Maggie shot back, laughing.

'Thanks a lot, friend. Anyway, getting back to the play, you know it pretty well too, and that's going to be a decided advantage when you start designing the sets.'

'You do realize I'm very worried about this whole project, don't you, Sam? I can't imagine how I ever let you talk me into it. I've never designed a stage set in my life.'

'But you have designed some beautiful rooms, especially lately, and anyway there's a first time for everything. You'll be okay, you'll do fine.'

'I wish I felt as confident as you sound. To tell you the truth, I'm not sure where to begin. I read the play through again last night and my mind went totally blank. In fact, I balked at the project. Are you certain there's no one else to do the sets for you?'

'There isn't, Maggie. Besides, you're only suffering from a touch of stage fright, and that's quite normal. Look, you'll be fine as soon as you pick up your pencil and start sketching. *Trust me.*'

'I'm not so sure I should do that, Sam. When I've

trusted you in the past it's only got me into a heap of trouble.'

'No, it hasn't,' Samantha countered and pushed her chair away from the card table. She stood up, walked across the stage, gesturing as she did.

'You'll have to create some sort of major scenic backdrop here, Mag, and the furniture must be representative of the period. Early American, obviously. But you're an expert on furniture, so I don't really know why I'm even mentioning it.'

Samantha swung to face her old friend. 'I see something dramatic in my mind's eye, something really unusual for the backdrop. Black and white, maybe even a few greys, something like a painting in grisaille. What do you think?'

Maggie rose and went to join her, nodding as she did. 'Yes!' she exclaimed, sounding excited by the project for the first time. 'I know exactly what you mean. It needs to be stark. Bleak almost. Certainly sombre, very eye-catching as well. I think the set has to be a little offbeat, not the usual thing. Let's take the audience by surprise.' Maggie raised a brow. 'Don't you agree?'

Samantha grinned at her. 'I sure do and I knew you'd catch the bug, once I got that clever little brain of yours working. You're so talented, Maggie, and very imaginative, and I'm certain you'll come up with exactly the right thing.'

'I hope so, I'd hate to let you down –' She broke off, looking thoughtful, then added, 'You know, I think I'll drive into New York later this week, pick up some books on theatrical design and stage sets.'

'Yes, do that. No, wait a minute, there's no need to go into Manhattan. Try the bookstore in Washington and the one in Kent. I know they're both well stocked. They have everything from soup to nuts.'

Maggie laughed, as always amused by her friend's colourful expressions, as she had been since their college days.

The two women stood centre stage, discussing ideas for the backdrop and the sets for a few minutes longer. At one moment Maggie went and got her notebook, began to sketch rapidly, all the time listening to Samantha and nodding.

Both women were forty-three and good-looking, but they were strikingly different in appearance and personality.

Samantha Matthews was of medium height and slim, with prematurely silver hair cut short with a fringe. The silver colour did not seem at all ageing since she had a youthfully pretty face and a fresh complexion. Her large eyes, set widely apart, were dark brown and full of soul.

Energetic, enthusiastic and gregarious, she had an outgoing personality and a friendly nature. Somewhat given to taking control, she liked to be in charge. Nonetheless, she was kind, good hearted and easy to get along with.

In contrast, Maggie Sorrell was tall, willowy, with the brightest of light blue eyes that were, at times, highly appraising. Her thick mane of chestnut hair was shot through with auburn lights and she wore it brushed back and falling to her shoulders. Although her face was a little angular and arresting rather than pretty, she was attractive and appealing in her looks.

Maggie had a fluidity and a gracefulness when she moved and she appeared to take things at a more leisurely pace. But she had as much energy and vitality as Samantha. Very simply, her style was slightly different. It was calm, controlled, and she was the quieter and more reserved of the two. And yet she was a vibrant woman, full of life and optimism.

Even in their style of dressing they were true to themselves. Tonight Samantha wore what she termed her uniform: well-tailored blue jeans, a white cotton shirt, a black gabardine blazer with brass buttons, and highly polished black oxfords with white socks.

Maggie, who tended to be less tailored, was dressed in a full, three-quarter length skirt made of brown suede, matching suede boots, a cream silk shirt and a brown cashmere stole flung over her shoulders.

Both women had a casual style about them which reflected an understanding of clothes and what suited them; it also bespoke their privileged backgrounds.

Best friends since college days, they had remained close even though they had been separated by thousands of miles for many years. They had managed to meet quite frequently, at least twice a year, and they had spoken to each other on the phone every week for as long as they could remember. Maggie had moved to Connecticut eight months ago, after a dreadful upheaval in her life, and they had become inseparable again.

The banging of a door at the back of the theatre startled both women, made them jump. Automatically they swung around, peering into the dimly lit auditorium.

'Oh, it's only Tom Cruise,' Samantha said immediately, a look of pleasure settling on her face. She waved with a certain eagerness to the man walking down the aisle towards the proscenium.

'*Tom Cruise*,' Maggie hissed, grasping Samantha's arm, following the direction of her gaze. 'Why didn't you tell me, for God's sake! Has he moved here? Is he taking an interest in the theatre group? Oh my God, I hope he's not slumming, doing a part in the play just for kicks. I'll never be able to design the sets! Not with a real pro around.'

Samantha burst out laughing. She said, in a low voice, 'As far as I know, Mr Cruise is still living in Westport. The guy walking towards us could be him though, and that's why I call him Tom Cruise.'

Maggie let go of Samantha's arm as the young man walked across the stage to join them.

'Sorry I'm late,' he said to Samantha, stretching out his hand, shaking hers.

'No problem,' Samantha answered. 'Come and meet my friend. Maggie, this is Jake Cantrell. Jake, this is Margaret Anne Sorrell, usually known as Maggie. She's an interior designer and will be designing our sets. Maggie, Jake's a genius with lighting and special effects. I hope he's going to become part of our little group and work with us. We certainly need a lighting expert of his calibre.'

Jake gave Samantha a small smile that hinted of shyness and then turned to Maggie. 'I'm very pleased to meet you,' he said politely and offered her his hand.

Maggie took it. His hand was cool, his grasp firm. 'I'm happy to meet you too,' she murmured.

They stood staring at each other.

Maggie thought how extremely good-looking he was, realizing at once that he was completely unaware that he was. He's a troubled man, she thought, recognizing the sadness in his eyes.

Jake was thinking that he'd never met a woman like this in his life, so beautifully groomed and well put together. He was suddenly awed by this woman who was looking at him so thoughtfully through her cool, intelligent eyes.

CHAPTER
3

THE THREE OF THEM sat down at the table on the stage and Samantha handed Jake a copy of the play.

'Thanks,' he said, glancing at it, then looking up at her as she continued, 'As you can see we're doing *The Crucible*, and I think you should read it as soon as possible.' She flashed him a vivid smile, and added, 'Basically, the meeting tonight is for us to become acquainted. I was hoping the three of us could get together again later this week, maybe on Friday or Saturday, to have our first detailed discussion about the scenery and the lighting. By then you'll have a better understanding of what's required.'

'I know the play,' Jake replied, giving her a pointed look. 'And very well. From high school. I also saw a revival of it a few years ago. I've always liked Arthur Miller.'

If Samantha was surprised to hear this she certainly disguised it. Merely nodding, she murmured, 'That's great. Obviously I'm delighted you know the play; it'll save us a lot of time in the long run.'

'I've never done any stage work before, as I told you when you phoned,' Jake said. 'But what's required for this play in particular is real mood, that I *do* know. All stage lighting should underscore the meaning of the drama, the scenes being acted, and create an atmosphere. In *The Crucible* it should be one of . . . mystery. Deep mystery, I think. And revelation . . . impending revelation. It's important to introduce a sense of time as well as place. In this instance, Salem, Massachusetts in the seventeenth century. Candles are going to be important, as are special effects. It's necessary to simulate dawn and nighttime. I remember a night-time scene in the wood. You'll need interesting combinations of light and shadow –' He stopped, wondering if he'd said too much – even worse, made a fool of himself.

Jake sat back in his chair and looked at the women. They were both staring at him intently. He felt himself flush and experienced a surge of acute embarrassment.

Maggie, who had been observing him closely and giving him her entire attention, sensed that he was suddenly feeling uncomfortable, although she wasn't sure why. But wishing to put him at ease, she said swiftly, 'You've hit it right on the mark, Jake. I'm fairly familiar with the play myself, but I know the scenery is going to be tough for me to do. This is *my* first stab at theatrical design. Like you I'm a bit of a novice. Maybe we'll be able to help each other as we go along.'

Smiling, Maggie finished, 'Samantha has a good point about meeting again later in the week, once we've both had a chance to refresh our memories about the play. I'm available either Friday or Saturday.' She glanced at Samantha and then back at him. 'Which day do you both prefer?'

'Saturday,' Samantha answered.

Jake was silent. An unfamiliar discomfort had settled over him. They were taking it for granted he was going to get involved with their drama group, but he still wasn't sure that he would. Or whether he even wanted to. He wondered if he'd said too much a moment ago, if he had led them to believe he intended to participate.

'Would Friday be better for you, Jake?' Maggie asked.

He shook his head. 'No, I don't think so. I –' He cut himself off abruptly, suddenly wary of making any kind of commitment to them. It might take up too much of his time; after all, he did have a business to run these days. Also, he was beginning to feel a bit out of his depth with these two women. They were so sure of themselves, were from another world, one he didn't know at all. And there was another thing: it seemed to him that they took their amateur theatrical group very seriously. Certainly they were determined to put on a good production, he could tell that. He knew Samantha Matthews was a perfectionist, his client in Washington had indicated that only the other day. It was apparent to him that she would be a hard taskmaster, very demanding. Better to skip it, he thought.

Clearing his throat, he looked across at Samantha and said, 'I agreed to come tonight because I'm always interested in extending my knowledge, so the idea of designing stage lighting appealed to me. But I have the feeling you want a real commitment from me, Samantha, and I can't give you that. What I mean is, I'm very busy with my electrical business. I work late most nights –'

'Oh, Jake, don't be so hasty,' Samantha interrupted. 'Maggie and I are also up to our necks with work. We've all got to earn a living, you know.'

Once again she offered him that vivid smile of hers, and added, 'Whatever you might think, you wouldn't be making such a huge commitment. Not really. Once you'd created the lighting effects you wouldn't have anything else to do. I'd take it from there. I've got several good stagehands to help me and an electrician as well.'

'Lighting isn't easy,' he answered. 'In fact, it's very complicated and especially so for *this* play.'

'You're absolutely correct,' Maggie interjected. 'But I do wish you'd reconsider. From what Sam's told me about your work at the Bruce house, you really do know what you're doing. Look, I know how you feel, I just started a new business myself a few months ago, and I'm totally committed to it. Nonetheless, I think I'll learn a lot from this little theatrical venture.' She smiled at him winningly.

He looked at her, looked right into her eyes, and he felt the hairs on the back of his neck bristling. Maggie Sorrell was not pretty in the given sense. But there was something about her that went beyond mere prettiness. She was arresting, intriguing, the kind of woman a man would look at twice. She had an elegance that had nothing to do with her clothes, but with herself. He felt oddly drawn to her. Instantly, he pulled back. He had never known a woman like this; he was not sure he wanted to.

Since he had remained mute, Maggie continued talking. 'You did say yourself that initially you thought you'd learn something. Actually, Jake, we'll both benefit, and in innumerable ways. For instance, there's the publicity. We'll get quite a lot, and that can't be bad for your business or mine. Anyway, I've come to realize that whatever I'm doing I'm usually meeting a potential client somewhere along the line.'

'Bravo! Said like a true professional!' Samantha exclaimed. 'And Maggie's correct, Jake, you can profit from this in a variety of different ways.'

When he still said nothing, she pressed, 'What do you have to lose?'

Hesitating for a moment longer, he finally said in a quiet voice, 'It's the time that's involved, I can't let my business suffer.'

'None of us can,' Maggie pointed out. 'Come on, Jake, give it a try. I am. The whole project is challenging and I love a challenge, don't you?' Not waiting for his answer, she said, 'In any case, I think we'll have a lot of fun together.'

Before he could stop himself he agreed. He

wondered what he was doing, making such a commitment. To cover himself, he added swiftly, 'If it gets to be too much, gets in the way of my work, I'll have to quit. You do understand that, don't you?'

'Of course,' Samantha replied.

'What about the next meeting, Jake? Do you prefer Friday or Saturday?' Maggie asked.

'Saturday's definitely better,' Jake told her. 'I'm working late on Friday, and on Saturday morning. Can we make it Saturday afternoon? Late afternoon?'

'Fine by me,' Maggie murmured.

'You've got a deal!' Samantha cried, her voice suddenly full of excitement. 'We're going to make a great team! And you'll enjoy it, Jake, you'll see. It's going to be a gratifying experience. Incidentally, I was impressed with what you said earlier, about the lighting for the play. Your ideas are brilliant. Personally, I think you've already got the lighting licked.'

'I hope so,' he replied, trying not to look pleased at her compliment. 'I've always found that play very powerful.'

'Yes, it is, and frightening in a sense, when you think it all hinges on lies – the terrible lies people tell,' Maggie remarked.

It was a few minutes before nine when Jake walked back into his kitchen, and he realized how hungry he was as he opened the fridge door and took out a cold beer.

After swallowing a few gulps, he went through into the living room, draped his sports jacket over a chair back and returned to the kitchen. Within a few minutes he had opened a can of corned beef and a jar of pickles and made himself a sandwich.

Carrying the plate and the beer back into the living room, he put them on the small glass coffee table, sat down, picked up the remote control and flicked on the television. He ate his sandwich and drank his beer, staring at the set. It was a sitcom on one of the networks and he wasn't paying much attention.

Jake was preoccupied with the drama group, *The Crucible* and the two women he had left a short while before. They were opposites, but they were both very nice and he liked them. And so he had let himself be persuaded to do the lighting for the play. Now he wished he hadn't agreed. He had done so against his better judgement and instinctively he knew it was going to be more trouble than it was worth. Why did I let myself get swept up into this? he asked himself yet again.

Suddenly impatient with the television and with himself, he flicked off the set and leaned back in the chair, taking an occasional swallow of beer.

After a moment Jake got up, walked over to the window, stood looking out at the night sky. He wondered what she was really like, Maggie Sorrell, but he figured he would never get to know her well enough to find out.

CHAPTER
4

MAGGIE SORRELL AWAKENED with a start. Reaching out, she turned on the bedside lamp and looked at the alarm clock. It was three-thirty.

Groaning to herself, she doused the light, slid down under the covers and attempted to go back to sleep. But her mind raced when she began to think about the living room and library of the house in Roxbury she was redecorating for a client. Fabric patterns, carpet swatches, paint colours and wood finishes swirled around in her head.

She finally gave up trying to envision a scheme. Jake Cantrell kept intruding into her thoughts. There was something about him that was appealing, very engaging, and of course he was stunning looking. But he doesn't know it, not really, she thought again, as she had a few hours ago. And then remembering the sadness she had detected in his light green eyes, she wondered what had gone awry in *his* life.

Obviously someone had hurt Jake Cantrell and very badly. She recognized that look only too well. The shell-shocked look she called it.

A woman did him in, Maggie thought, still focusing on Jake. She sighed to herself. Women. Men. What they did to each other in the name of love was diabolical. It bordered on the criminal. She ought to know, it had been done to her.

Mike Sorrell had destroyed her just as surely as if he had stuck a knife in her. But then he'd been killing her soul for years, hadn't he?

The big upheaval had happened two years ago, but the memory of it was still there. Although most of the pain had receded, there were moments when it came rushing back, took her by surprise with its intensity. She tried to squash the bad memories but they seemed determined to linger.

I'll be forty-four next month, she thought. *Forty-four.* It didn't seem possible. Time had rushed by with the speed of light. Where had all the years gone? Well, she knew the answer to that. Mike Sorrell had devoured them. She had devoted most of her life to Michael William Sorrell, attorney-at-law by profession, and to their twins, Hannah and Peter, college students both, soon to be twenty-one years old.

The three of them were gone from her life and she had learned to live without them. But it still pained her when she thought of the twins. They had sided with their father, even though she had done nothing wrong. He was the guilty party. But then he was Mr Money Bags and that apparently carried weight with them.

How terrible it was to know your children were greedy, avaricious and selfish, when you'd tried so hard to bring them up right, to instil proper values in them. But there it was. They had proved to her that she had failed with them.

In taking his side they had destroyed something fundamental deep within her. She had borne them, brought them up, looked after them when they were sick. She had always been there for them and guided them all of their lives. What they had done to her was rotten, in her opinion. They had flung all that caring back in her face. Flung her love for them back at her, as if it were meaningless.

In a sense, their cold-hearted defection had stunned her more than Mike's ugly betrayal of her. He'd dumped her when she was nearly forty-two for a younger woman, a woman of twenty-seven who was a lawyer in another Chicago law firm.

But I survived, Maggie reminded herself, thanks mainly to Samantha. And myself, of course.

It was Samantha who had reached out to her two years ago, that awful day in May, the day of her birthday when she had finally admitted to herself that she would be spending it alone.

Hannah and Peter were both attending North-western, but were far too busy with their own lives to make time for their mother's birthday celebration. And their father had left that morning on a business trip without wishing her a happy birthday. Apparently he hadn't even remembered it.

That May morning, sitting alone in the kitchen of their apartment on Lake Shore Drive, she had felt totally, completely alone. And without her husband and children she was. Her parents were dead and she had been an only child. That special morning she had felt something else – abandoned, cast aside, of no use to anyone anymore. Even now, so long after, she was unable to pinpoint her exact feelings, but she had been disturbed, she knew that.

When the phone had rung and she had answered, had heard Samantha singing 'Happy birthday', she had burst into tears. Between sobs she had explained that she was spending her birthday alone because the kids didn't have time for her and Mike had gone away on a business trip.

'Pack a bag, get out to O'Hare and take a plane to New York! *Immediately*!' Samantha had exclaimed. 'I'll book us into the Carlyle. I have some pull there, I can usually get rooms. I'm taking you out on the town tonight. Somewhere posh and smart. So pack your fanciest gear.'

When she had tried to protest, Samantha had said, 'I'm not listening to your excuses. And I won't take no for an answer. There's a plane leaving every hour on the hour. Just get on one and get yourself to New York. *Pronto, pronto, pronto*, honey. I'll meet you at the hotel.'

True to her word, Samantha had been there when she arrived, full of warmth and love, sympathy and support. They had enjoyed their two days together in

Manhattan, doing a little shopping and eating at nice restaurants. A Broadway play and a trip to the Metropolitan Museum had been mandatory; they had also found time to talk endlessly, reminiscing about their days at Bennington College, when they first met, and their lives thereafter.

Samantha had married several years after Maggie. Her husband had been a British journalist based in New York. She and Angus McAllister had tied the knot when she was twenty-five and he was thirty-one. It had been a very happy marriage, but Angus had been tragically killed in a plane crash five years later, en route to the Far East on an assignment.

It was only a few months after this that Samantha, who was childless, moved back to Washington, Connecticut, where her parents had long owned a country house they used at weekends. Heartbroken though she had been, she had managed eventually to get her grief under control. But she had never remarried, although there had been several men in her life in the intervening years.

At one moment, during the birthday visit, Maggie had asked Samantha why this was so. Samantha had shaken her head and said, in her colourful way, 'Ain't found the right man, honey chile. I'm looking to fall head over heels in love, the way I did with Angus. I want my stomach to lurch and my knees to wobble.' She had laughed, and finished, 'I want to be swept off my feet, into his arms, into his bed and his life forever. It *must* be like that for me or it won't work. And I'm still waiting to meet him.'

Later, on the plane going back to Chicago, Maggie

had admitted to herself that her marriage to Mike was growing more and more unsatisfactory with the passing of every day. She did not know what to do about it. He did. A day later he returned from his trip. He walked into the apartment, announced he was leaving her for another woman, and walked right out again.

Once the shock had subsided and she had recovered her equilibrium to a degree, she had set about cleaning up the mess his unexpected departure had created.

Divorce proceedings were started, the apartment went on the market, and once it was sold she moved back east, back to her home town. New York.

She had lived there for six months in a small, rented studio. Her parents were already dead, she had no family, and she'd lost touch with all of her old friends from her youth. It was a lonely life for her.

It didn't take much persuasion on Samantha's part to get her to start looking at houses in the northwestern part of Connecticut.

Samantha also talked her into working as an interior designer again. Some years ago, she had been the junior member of a successful Chicago decorating firm and had loved every moment working there. She had finally given up her job because of pressure from Mike.

But she did what her best friend suggested and hung out her shingle, once she was installed in her small Connecticut colonial in Kent. The house, a little gem in her opinion, was only a few miles from Washington, where Samantha lived.

Thanks to Samantha's many contacts, design work had started to come Maggie's way quickly. They were small jobs. However, they had helped to pull her back into the swing of decorating, and the money she earned paid part of the mortgage.

Samantha, the eternal optimist, kept telling her a really big job would come her way one day soon. Maggie believed her because she was also an optimist.

Soon Maggie began to accept that sleep would be evasive for the rest of the night. Putting on the light, she peered at the alarm clock again and decided to get up. It was just turning four o'clock and she often rose at this hour. She accomplished a lot before eight whenever she did.

An hour later Maggie sat at her desk, sipping a mug of coffee. She was dressed and made up and ready for the day ahead. Later in the morning she would be driving over to Samantha's studio in Washington to look at her latest handpainted fabrics for a bedroom she was doing in New Preston. Then she would be presenting the scheme for the library to the owner of the house in Roxbury. Pulling the swatches and samples together for this room was the order of the day and of vital importance.

Maggie began to assemble the small samples from various canvas bags at her feet. There was a variety of different greens and reds, colours the owner wanted, but not one of them was pleasing to her. Most of the reds were too bright, the greens too pale. Something sombre, she muttered under her breath. And then for a reason she couldn't explain she thought of *The Crucible*, and of the meeting last night.

Again Jake Cantrell insinuated himself into her thoughts. If she were honest with herself, she'd have to admit she felt rather foolish, believing as she had, if only for a few moments, that he was Tom Cruise. But Samantha had sounded so convincing when she'd spotted him coming down the aisle of the auditorium. He'd taken them both by surprise when he started to talk about his ideas for the lighting. It was obvious to her from that moment on that he was knowledgeable about his work, and most likely as brilliant as Samantha said. Of course, you never knew with Sam. She had always liked a pretty face, Maggie thought, as she shuffled the samples on the desk, and then she stopped and sat back in her chair, staring into space. 'But he's too young for her,' she muttered aloud. And for you too, she added to herself silently.

CHAPTER
5

JAKE HEARD THE PHONE ringing as he stepped out of the shower. He reached for a towel, partially dried himself and pulled on his terry-cloth robe.

Walking into the bedroom he heard Maggie Sorrell's voice saying goodbye. The answering machine clicked off; he depressed the button and played the message back.

Her voice filled the room. 'Jake, this is Maggie Sorrell. I've just been hired to do a big job in Kent. A farm. It's a beautiful old place but it needs a lot of work. The grounds are superb. I was wondering if you would be interested in doing the electrical work? Interiors and exteriors. Please call me. I'm here at home.' She then repeated the number she'd given him last Saturday at the drama group meeting.

Jake sat down on the bed and played the message again. He loved her voice. It was light, musical, cultured. It suited her. He had met her three times now at meetings about *The Crucible*, and he realized that his attraction to her was powerful. He thought about her a lot. But he had no intention of doing anything about her. She'd never be interested in him.

He would like to do the electrical work, though. The major job he had been doing in Washington was just about completed, and he and his crew would finish in the next couple of days. With four men on the payroll he had to pull in as many jobs as possible to keep them busy. Two were married and had families to support, and he felt a great sense of responsibility.

He picked up the phone to call Maggie back, and then he dropped the receiver in the cradle. He did not want to seem too anxious. Then again, he always felt a bit nervous around her.

Returning to the bathroom, he combed his wet hair and finished his ablutions, then went to get dressed, pulled on blue jeans and a sweater.

Fifteen minutes later he sat down at the desk in the small room at the back of the house, which he used as an office. Pulling the phone towards him, he dialled Maggie's number.

She answered immediately. 'Hello?'

'It's Jake, Maggie.'

'Hello, Jake, you got my message?'

'Yes, I did. I was in the shower when you called.' He wondered why he'd told her that. Rushing on, he continued quickly, 'The farm job sounds interesting. Where is it exactly?'

'It's not too far from Kent, near Bull's Bridge Corner, actually. It's a pretty property and the house has great charm.'

'Is it really a big job?'

'I think so. To be honest with you, Jake, the entire farmhouse needs rewiring, and it needs remodelling and restoring. It hasn't been touched in thirty years, in my opinion anyway. The woman who's bought it, my client, wants air conditioning and central heating systems put in, all new appliances in the kitchen, and she wants to build a laundry. Then there are the grounds. The exterior lighting will be extensive. She wants to build a pool and patio, oh, and there's an old cottage to be remodelled for guests, as well as a caretaker's apartment over the cottage.' She laughed. 'So I guess it is a huge job.'

'It sounds like it to me, Maggie. What are we looking at? About six or seven months' work?'

'Probably. Maybe a bit longer. Can you handle it?'

'Yes, I'm pretty sure I can. And thanks for thinking of me.'

'Samantha's always said you're the best, and yesterday I saw the work you've done in the Washington house, and on the grounds there. I was very impressed.'

'Thanks. When can I see the farm? I'd like to, before I commit to it.'

'We could go over there later this week.'

'Okay.'

'How does Friday sound? That's the fourteenth of April.'

'Great. What time?'

'Could you do it around eight?'

'Sure thing. Whereabouts is it?'

'It's hard for me to give you the right directions . . . it's up a lot of twisting roads. I think we should meet at my house, since you know where it is, and we can go from here. It's easier and it'll save time.'

'I'll be there at eight sharp. And Maggie?'

'Yes, Jake?'

'Thanks for thinking of me.'

After hanging up, Jake wrote the appointment in the small pocket diary he carried around with him, and also put it in the agenda on the desk. Then he got up and left the house.

As he walked out to the pick-up truck it struck him that perhaps he hadn't been so foolish after all, getting involved with the drama group. It looked as if he was getting a job because of it. But he knew the real reason he had become involved with the theatre group. It was because of her, of course. He had done it because of Maggie Sorrell.

He sat at the steering wheel without moving for a few seconds, bracing himself. He was on his way to an appointment, and he wasn't looking forward to it.

Amy Cantrell stood in the centre of the living room of her apartment, looking around slowly, all of a sudden noticing the untidiness of the place. Dismay swamped her.

She had managed to talk Jake into coming over

tonight, for the first time in months, and she knew he would be furious. He loathed mess and disorder. He was as neat as a pin himself, and had been as long as she had known him, which was forever. Her lack of organization and her untidiness had been a bone of contention between them. She never understood how she could create chaos in a room within seconds. She never meant to, it just happened.

Shaking her head and frowning, she began quickly to pick up the newspapers and magazines scattered all over the coffee table and on the floor underneath. She put them on a chair, plumped up the cushions on the sofa, and took the newspapers out to the kitchen.

When she saw the dirty dishes in the sink she groaned. She had forgotten about them. Flinging down the papers angrily, she opened the dishwasher; it was stacked to the brim and had not been turned on. Everything was dirty. Trying to stack more items into it and moving quickly, she dropped a mug. It shattered.

The phone rang shrilly. She grabbed it. 'Hello?'

'Amy, it's me. Has he arrived yet?'

'No, Mom, he's not coming until after eight.'

'Why so late, Amy?'

'I don't know. He works, Mom.'

'Tell him about the alimony. That you want alimony.'

'Mom, I gotta go. Honestly I do. I'm trying to tidy up here. Jake hates mess.'

'So what do you care? He left you.'

'I gotta go, Mom. 'Bye.' She hung up before her mother could say another word.

Moving across the kitchen floor in the direction of the dishwasher, she crushed the shards of pottery from the broken mug under her feet. Amy looked down, bit her lip. She went to find the brush and dustpan; she was on the verge of tears.

For the next few minutes she attempted to bring order to the kitchen before going through into the bedroom. The bed was unmade, as it usually was these days. The mere thought of making it overwhelmed her, and defeated by the domestic chores which needed doing, she scurried into the bathroom.

After washing her face and cleaning her teeth, she combed her pale blonde hair. It hung listlessly around her face.

Amy Cantrell sighed as she regarded herself in the mirror. She wondered how she could make herself look better, and reached for the Cover Girl foundation, patted some of it on her face and added powder. Once she had highlighted her cheekbones with the blush-on, she outlined her mouth with pale pink lipstick.

The image of herself in the mirror infuriated her. She didn't look any better than she had a few seconds ago. Tears flooded her eyes. She was a mess. The apartment was a mess. She had never known what to do about either.

Her friend Mandy had once offered to show her how to use cosmetics, but she had never taken her up on it. She wondered why. As for the state of the house, there was never any time, and the more she did to clean it up, the more chaotic it became. Reaching for a tissue, she blew her nose and wiped her eyes. It just wasn't fair. Other people seemed to get through life so easily, so flawlessly. All she could do was stumble along, dragging mess in her wake.

The doorbell rang, making her jump.

My God, was he here already! She hurried out into the little entrance foyer, realizing, as she went to open the door, that she was still wearing the cotton house-coat she had donned earlier when she had started the housework.

'Who is it?' she asked through the door.

'It's Jake.'

Glancing down at her grubby housecoat, she made a face and then opened the door.

'Hi, Amy,' he said, coming in.

'Hi, Jake,' she echoed, closing the door, trailing after him lethargically.

'How've you been? All right, I guess.'

'I guess. And you?'

'Busy. With the business.'

'Oh.'

Jake glanced around and then sat down on one of the chairs.

Amy could not help but notice the distaste on his face. She winced inside. He had always been par-ticular about the apartment, and his appearance. She glanced at him obliquely. He looked impeccable tonight. As he always had. Always did. He was wear-ing a beige turtleneck sweater and dark blue jeans with a navy blazer. His boots shone, his hair shone, so did his teeth and his face. He looked brand spank-ing new, like a freshly minted coin.

More conscious than ever that she looked awful, if

not worse than awful, Amy simply sat down on the chair opposite and smiled at him.

Jake cleared his throat. 'You said you had to see me. You were very insistent. What do you want to talk about, Amy?'

'The divorce.'

'We've discussed it so much we've worn the subject out,' he answered in an even tone.

'I just want to be sure you're sure, Jake.'

'I am, Amy. I'm sorry, but there's no going back.'

Her pale blue eyes filled. She blinked the tears away, pushed her hair out of her face. Trying to get a grip on her emotions, she took several deep breaths. 'Well, I have been to see the lawyer. Finally. I'm sure you're pleased about that.'

'When did you go?' he asked.

'Yesterday.'

'I see. I'm glad you did. We should get this over, Amy, so that we can settle everything.'

'He asked me if we'd tried to solve our problems. I told him yes, but that it wasn't any good, that it wouldn't work. Are you really sure, Jake? Maybe we should try again.'

'I can't, Amy. Honestly, honey, I can't. It's finished.'

The tears rolled down her cheeks.

'Oh, Amy, please don't cry.'

'I still love you, Jake.'

He said nothing.

'All the years,' she said, staring hard at him. 'We've known each other since we were twelve. It's a long, long time.'

'I know. And maybe that's the problem. Perhaps

we know each other too well. We've become like brother and sister. Listen to me, Amy, you've got to face up to the fact that our marriage is over, and it's been over for years and years.' He cleared his throat and finished gently, 'You just never noticed.'

'I don't know what I'm going to do without you,' she wept.

'You're going to be fine. I know you are.'

'I don't think I am, Jake. Would you get me a glass of water, please? Do you want a beer?'

'No, thanks. I'll get the water for you.' Jake manoeuvred himself through the living room into the kitchen, and he could not help noticing how dirty the apartment was. He bent down, picked up the broken mug and put it on the counter top. His eyes fell on the dishwasher jammed with dirty dishes and the sink piled even higher, and he grimaced. Once he had found a relatively clean glass in the cupboard, he rinsed it, filled it with cold water and took it to her.

Amy thanked him, sat sipping it for a few moments, staring at him over the rim of the glass. She was trying to think of something to say to him, but no words would come, and her head was empty of thoughts. All she really wanted was for him to come back to her. Then she wouldn't feel so lonely.

Jake said, 'I'll have to be going, Amy, I've work to do tonight.'

'You're not dressed like you're going to work!' she exclaimed, giving him a furious look, suddenly filled with jealousy.

'Paperwork, Amy, I've loads of it.'

'Do you want me to come and help you?'

'No, no,' he said hurriedly, standing up. 'But thanks for the offer.' He began to edge his way to the hall.

Amy put the glass down and stood up. She followed him to the front door. 'The lawyer says I'm entitled to alimony,' she announced.

'That's no problem, Amy, and it never was. I always told you I would look after you.'

'Then stay with me.'

'I can't. What I meant was I'd look after you financially. Tell the lawyer to go ahead and talk to my lawyer. Serve me with papers, Amy. Let's get this over with.'

She did not answer him.

'So long,' he said. 'I'll talk to you soon.' When she chose not to answer him he simply closed the door behind him quietly and left. Poor Amy.

CHAPTER
6

O N FRIDAY MORNING Jake set out for Maggie Sorrell's house in Kent.

He knew where it was. He had gone there with Samantha Matthews the previous week to have another meeting about the lighting for *The Crucible*. It was not too far from where he lived, on the other side of town, half way down Route 7.

As he pulled out of his yard and headed up Route 341 in the direction of the town centre in Kent, Jake thought what a glorious morning it was, the way you always hoped an April day would be. It was crisp and dry, with bright sunlight and a vivid blue sky filled with puffed white clouds, the kind of day that made him feel good to be alive. Opening the window of the pick-up, he took a few deep breaths of the pure clean air.

Jake was finally feeling better in spirits. After his meeting with Amy on Tuesday night, he had been depressed for almost two days. She always managed to drag him down, to drain the energy out of him with her negative personality and her total lack of direction and purpose.

Sometimes Jake wondered how Amy managed to keep her job in the store, where she had worked for a number of years; it baffled him. It was a bath speciality store, selling everything for the bathroom from towels to accessories. Seemingly the owner liked her enough to keep her on, despite the constant mistakes she made.

Jake glanced out of the pick-up's window, noted that the light was crystalline today. Perfect. He wished he had time to get out his paints this weekend, but he knew it was not possible. He had paperwork to finish; also, if he was lucky, and Maggie hired him, he would have to start analysing the electrical work required at the farm.

He had allowed himself half an hour to get to Maggie's house, but since there was no traffic he arrived there fifteen minutes early. He parked in the back yard and walked towards the kitchen door, noting how pristine and well-cared-for the traditional Connecticut colonial looked. The clapboard walls were painted white and all of the shutters were dark green.

Before he reached the kitchen door, Maggie opened it. She stood there on the step, smiling at him.

The minute he saw her his chest tightened and he felt himself grow hot. To cover his nervousness, his sudden confusion, he coughed several times, then murmured, 'Good morning, I'm afraid I'm early.'

She stretched out her hand. He took it in his. She said, 'Good morning, Jake. That's no problem – I've been up since dawn. Come on in and have a cup of coffee before we leave.' She smiled at him once more and extracted her hand.

He didn't want to let go of it, but he did. 'Thanks, coffee would be good.' He followed her into the immaculate kitchen, stood there glancing around, feeling slightly awkward.

Maggie said, 'Sit down, Jake. You take your coffee black, if I remember correctly, with one sugar.' One of her dark brows lifted questioningly.

'That's right, thanks,' he answered, and took a seat at the old pine table at one end of the kitchen, noticing that it had been set for breakfast for two.

She moved past him, and he caught a faint whiff of shampoo in her thick, luxuriant hair, the scent of her perfume on her skin, something light and floral; he heard the gentle swish of her skirt against her boots, the tinkle of the gold bracelets she always seemed to wear on one of her slender wrists.

Maggie moved around the kitchen quickly, but with the gracefulness he had noticed before. She was tall and slender, full of life and energy; he could not take his eyes off her. Eventually he did so, realizing he was staring.

Jake looked away quickly, let his eyes roam around the kitchen. He was struck by its singular charm, as

69

he had been last week. It was decorated to make a statement, but it was certainly not overdone. Everything was in the best of taste, from the white walls and cabinets and the terracotta tile floor, to the sparkle of copper.

Delicious smells were suddenly wafting on the air ... freshly baked bread, cooked apples and the hint of cinnamon mingled with the smell of coffee. He inhaled, then sniffed.

Maggie, who had turned around at this moment, said, 'I baked the bread earlier this morning and it's still warm. Would you like a slice? It's delicious, even though I say so myself.'

'I would, thanks very much. Can I do anything to help?' He started to rise.

'No, no, I can manage. The coffee's coming up, and then I'll bring the bread and honey.' As she spoke she glided across the kitchen floor, carrying the mugs of coffee, and a second later she was back again with the homemade bread, a honeycomb and a bowl of baked apples on a tray. She placed this in the centre of the table and sat down opposite him.

'I love baked apples,' she confided. 'Try one. They're great with a slice of warm bread and honey.'

'I will,' he said, as tongue-tied as ever, then thought to say thank you to her.

Maggie sipped her coffee and regarded him surreptitiously. He had helped himself to a baked apple and was eating it with relish, then he took a slice of the warm bread, spread it with butter and honey, took a bite.

He said, a second later, 'I haven't had homemade bread since I was a kid. It's nectar.'

'I know what you mean,' she answered, laughing, glad he was enjoying the breakfast. She had prepared it especially for him. It had struck her the other day that he probably didn't have very many proper meals. She knew from Samantha that he was single and lived alone in a charming white clapboard house on Route 341.

Maggie wondered if he had a girlfriend. Obviously he did. Looking the way *he* looked, and being as nice as he was, it was more than likely that women chased after him. She felt a little twinge of something, of what she was not sure. Envy? Jealousy? Or a bit of both? Of course he'd never be interested in her, so why daydream about him? Which is exactly what she had been doing since their first meeting. Actually, she couldn't get him out of her mind. The other night she had even had fantasies about making love with him, and now, as she remembered those images, she felt herself flushing.

Maggie stood up swiftly and hurried over to the counter, convinced that her face had turned scarlet. She was extremely conscious of Jake's presence in her kitchen. He seemed to fill it with his masculinity and strength. And his sexuality. She had not felt like this for years and years.

Pouring herself another cup of coffee, Maggie Sorrell cautioned herself to put Jake Cantrell out of her mind. At once. He was, after all, much younger than she. Beyond her reach in so many ways.

From the other side of the kitchen, Jake's eyes were

riveted on her. She was half turned away from him, so he was seeing her partly in profile, and he was struck yet again by her unusual beauty. There was a great deal of strength there, and yet she was the most feminine woman he had ever met, and vulnerable. He wanted to protect and cherish her. And love her. He already did. He had fallen for her the first night they met.

And he wanted to make love to her. He had done this so many times in his mind he was beginning to think it had really happened. But of course it hadn't; he fervently wished it had. Jake wanted to make love to her right now, had a terrible urge to get up and walk across the floor, take her in his arms and kiss her passionately. And he wanted to tell her exactly how he felt about her, but he didn't dare. It took all of his self-constraint to remain seated.

Jake picked up his coffee cup and discovered, to his dismay, that his hand shook slightly. Whenever he was near her she had the most extraordinary effect on him. I want her in every possible way, he thought, yet I know I can't have her. Oh God, I don't know what to do. What to do about her.

Maggie turned around.

Taken by surprise, he gaped at her.

She exclaimed, 'Are you all right, Jake?'

'Yes. Why?'

'You're looking a bit pale. And a bit odd.'

'I'm fine, thanks.'

'Would you like another cup of coffee?'

He shook his head. 'No, thanks. I'll finish this and then perhaps we'd better be on our way,' he answered, and was surprised his voice sounded so normal.

'I'll just go and get my things,' she said. 'I won't be a minute. Excuse me.'

Left alone he leaned back against the chair and exhaled. He wondered how he would be able to work with her on a continuing basis, and experienced a sudden surge of panic. For a split second he considered turning the job down if she offered it to him. Instantly he dismissed this idea. He needed another big job if his business was to grow and flourish. Not only that, he needed to be with her on a daily basis, needed to be near her however painful that might prove to be.

Jake Cantrell knew deep within himself that his wild imaginings about Maggie Sorrell would never come to pass. They were from wholly different worlds. She had never shown the remotest interest in him since the day they first met, other than to offer him this chance to bid on the electrical job at the farm she was decorating. It was obvious to him that his work and his knowledge about lighting impressed her. That would have to suffice.

Jake drove them to the farm in his pick-up truck, following Maggie's directions once they had left the centre of Kent.

Because he was so drawn to her, so smitten, and therefore needed her to think well of him, he was reluctant to say a word. He was afraid he might say the wrong thing. And so he sped to their destination in total silence.

For her part, Maggie believed he was naturally shy, a little withdrawn. Days ago she had decided he was a troubled man, one who had been badly hurt; he needed to be handled with gentleness, in her opinion.

Because of her own painful experiences, Maggie empathized with him and felt that she understood him without really knowing him. After two years of struggling with her own pain, she had finally managed to regain her self-confidence, but she was only too well aware that emotional damage could take a long time to heal. After Mike's rejection of her, and the break-up of their marriage, she had felt nothing for so long.

And so she began to talk to Jake quietly, discussing the play they were involved with and their designs for the scenery and lighting. She was able to draw him out a little; he became enthusiastic and articulate as he began to speak about the lighting techniques he was planning to use.

She listened attentively, making an occasional comment. But mostly she let him do the talking, recognizing that as he opened up to her he became more sure of himself. He was gaining confidence as he spoke fluently about his work.

In no time at all they were turning through white gates and heading up the driveway of Havers Hill, the farm Maggie had been hired to remodel, restore and decorate.

Jake parked near a big red barn and then walked around to help her get out of the pick-up. He gave her his hands and she took them. As she jumped down she lost her balance and stumbled against him. He caught her, held her in his arms for a brief moment, and she clung to him. They drew apart quickly, staring at each other self-consciously.

Maggie turned away, straightened her jacket to cover her sudden confusion, and then reached into the truck for her briefcase and handbag.

After she had moved away, Jake, swallowing hard, closed the door of the pick-up and swung around, glancing about him as he did.

The property was magnificent.

Well-kept green lawns sloped away from the drive, rolled as far as the eye could see. Beyond were pastures, and even farther beyond mountains partially encircled the property. Nearby, an old stone wall bordered a smaller lawn where a gazebo sat in the shade of an ancient gnarled maple, and the wall itself made a fitting backdrop for an English-style border of perennials.

He shaded his eyes with his hand. In the distance he could see an apple orchard. 'What a place!' he exclaimed. 'It's beautiful. I'd like to own something like this one day.'

'Then I'm sure you will,' she replied, smiling at him. 'If you want something badly enough you can usually get it, if you work hard at it, of course.'

Gesturing to a series of buildings just ahead of them, she went on, 'That's the caretaker's house over there, Jake, and the farmhouse is the bigger building to the right. Come on, I want to show you around.'

She began to walk rapidly towards the house, continuing, 'I told the caretaker, Mrs Briggs, that we'd be coming over, so the front door's open.' She glanced over her shoulder at him as she spoke.

Jake caught up with her and they went into the house together, their shoulders brushing in the narrow entrance.

Even though the lights were on, the hallway was dark and Jake blinked, adjusting his eyes to the murkiness of the interior.

'It's very old,' he said to Maggie, peering about, moving forward, looking inside several rooms that opened off the entrance hall.

'Yes, it is. About 1740 or 1750, somewhere thereabouts,' she told him. 'And it was furnished in Early American style; most authentically, in fact. Most of the furniture's been sold though. My client only wanted to keep a few choice pieces.'

'Think about it, Maggie, this house was built before the American Revolution. My God, what these walls could tell us if they could talk!'

Maggie laughed. 'I know exactly what you mean. I've often thought that myself. About other places I mean, especially in England and France.'

'Who owned the farm?' he asked, turning to her.

'A Mrs Stead. It had been in the Stead family for several hundred years. The last Mrs Stead died about a year and a half ago. No, two years ago, to be exact. She was very old, ninety-five when she died. Her English granddaughter inherited the property, but since she's a married woman with children and lives in London, obviously her life is on the other side of the Atlantic. So she put the property, the farmhouse and its contents on the market two years ago. She thought she'd sell Havers Hill immediately, because it is such an idyllic place. But the asking price was in the millions and it's no longer the 1980s. So naturally she didn't have any takers. She finally had to drop the price.'

Jake said, 'A lot of people who want to sell their weekend homes up here are beginning to realize the prices of the eighties are finished. Anyway, who finally bought it? Who's your client?'

'A married couple. Anne and Philip Lowden. They own an advertising agency on Madison Avenue. They live in Manhattan during the week, and wanted a retreat in the country. Anne fell in love with this place, especially the grounds. She came to me through a client in New Preston, whom I've done work for. Anne told me she liked my understated style. "No *nouveau riche* folderol for me," she said when we met. She didn't even bother to interview any other designers, just hired me to do it all. Anne wants me to modernize the farmhouse and the guest cottage.'

'The farmhouse certainly needs it,' Jake remarked, and turned to look at Maggie. 'Okay, where shall we start?'

'Let's go into the kitchen first. We can put our things there: it's the only place with any furniture in it anyway.'

Maggie led the way down a short corridor and into the kitchen. This was a medium-sized room with two adjoining pantries, a couple of small windows, and a beamed ceiling. It overlooked a vegetable garden, an old stone well and, to the right, a flower garden.

'A decent-sized room,' Jake commented as they

surveyed the kitchen together. 'But it's too dark, not much natural light coming in; you'll have to supplement it with really good artificial lighting.'

'I know,' Maggie murmured. 'And that's the problem with the whole house, Jake. It's so ... so gloomy. Personally, I find it quite depressing. I like airiness, pale colours, a sense of space. My aim is to get rid of the sombre feeling without having to put in too many additional windows. I don't want to kill the period look of the place. After all, it's one of the reasons my clients bought it. For its rustic charm and antiquity.'

'I understand.' Jake's eyes scanned the kitchen once more. He looked up at the ceiling and then walked around the room a few times, a thoughtful expression settling on his face.

Maggie placed her briefcase and handbag on the kitchen table, took out a notebook and made a few notations.

Jake said, after a moment, 'I don't think this room presents too many problems. We could use several large-sized ceiling fixtures, such as old lanterns, something like that, plus wall sconces, in order to introduce proper artificial light. And you might want to think about putting in a new kitchen door, one that has panes of glass in the upper portion.'

'Yes, I had thought of that ... it would let in additional natural daylight.'

'What about high hats? Would you or the clients object to a few in the ceiling?'

'No, since they're fairly unobtrusive. But can you do it?'

'I think so. I'll have to cut into the ceiling first, to investigate what's going on up there. But it shouldn't present any real problems. If I get the job, that is.'

Maggie stared at him, frowning slightly. 'Jake, surely you know you're going to get the job.'

'You might not like my estimate, it might not fit into your budget.'

'We'll make it fit into my budget, won't we, Jake?'

He gave her a long look and was silent for a few seconds. Then he said, 'I guess so. Have you found a contractor yet?'

'I'm thinking of hiring Ralph Sloane. He's done a bit of work for me, and I've seen some of his really huge jobs in the last few days. I like the way he operates, I like his style. Do you know him?'

'Yes, I've worked with him before. He's a good guy. Are you going to hire an architect? Or don't you plan on making structural changes?'

'The answer is yes to both of those questions, Jake. I met with Mark Payne the other day –'

'He's the best!' Jake cut in, sounding enthusiastic.

'That's what I thought. I've seen a lot of his work now, and he seems to be an expert when it comes to Colonial architecture. He'd like the job, I know that, and I was impressed with his ideas.' There was a small pause and then she finished, 'I think I'm putting together a good team, don't you?'

He glanced at her and nodded, gave her half a smile and then headed out of the kitchen. 'Shall we go through the rest of the house?'

'Yes, let's look at the rooms on this floor first.'

*　　　*　　　*

79

Three hours later they came out of the farmhouse together, blinking in the sunlight. Slowly they walked back to the pick-up truck.

Jake leaned against the hood, and said, 'It's a huge job, Maggie, bigger than I initially thought. The whole place needs rewiring. It obviously hasn't been touched in years. And there's so much else to do. We haven't even thought about the exterior lighting for the grounds.'

'I know.' She threw him a worried glance. 'You're not saying you don't want to tackle it, are you?'

'No. I want the job. I need it. As you know, I'm building a new business. Anyway, I like a challenge. And I want to work with you, Maggie.' He paused and stared into her face. Suddenly making a decision, taking control of the situation, he said in a firm voice, 'Let's go. I'll take you to lunch. I know a good place for a hamburger or a salad, whichever you prefer.'

'Good idea,' she responded. 'I'm starving.'

CHAPTER
7

WHEN JAKE KNOCKED on Maggie's kitchen door and there was no answer, he opened it and went inside.

She was nowhere in sight, so he wandered through the kitchen and into the small back hall, heading for her office. But he stopped at once, stood perfectly still, listening.

In the few weeks he had known Maggie Sorrell he had never seen her ruffled. Nor had he ever heard her raise her voice. But she was doing so now, obviously speaking on the phone in her office.

'He did it on purpose!' she exclaimed. 'Nothing you say will convince me otherwise. And he did it to hurt me. He simply doesn't want me there to celebrate with you.'

There was a sudden silence.

Jake guessed she was now listening to whoever it was on the other end of the line. Wanting to be polite, to make sure she was aware of his presence, he walked across the hall, knocked on the open door, poked his head around it and raised his hand in greeting.

Maggie stared at him so blankly he realized at once how preoccupied she was. But then she nodded quickly, acknowledging him.

He half smiled in return and ducked out. Swinging around, he headed towards the small sitting room opposite. After placing the envelope he was carrying on the coffee table, he walked over to the window and stood looking out of it at her garden, lost for a moment in his thoughts of her.

It was apparent to him that Maggie was not only angry but upset as well, and this disturbed him. He had become very protective of her.

Jake glanced at his watch. They had agreed to meet at six o'clock tonight, and as usual he was far too early. It seemed to him that he was continually ahead of himself whenever they had an appointment. He just couldn't help it. He wanted to be with her all the time; he hated it when they finished their work and he had to leave her.

They had known each other only five weeks yet it seemed so much longer to him. He had discovered that they were compatible, liked the same things. She loved music as much as he did and she was impressed with his knowledge of it. He enjoyed talking to her because she was so well informed; she was a news buff and, as he was, a great fan of CNN.

There were other things that he liked about her. She had a good sense of humour, laughed a lot, and she was a truly feminine woman. For all her ability and talent, strength and independence she was not hard. Just the opposite. He forever felt the urge to look after her.

Since his first visit to the farmhouse, two weeks ago now, Jake had begun to relax with her and, at the same time, he had acquired more self-confidence. In fact, ever since that Friday morning, when he had taken her for a hamburger in Kent, he had considered himself to be in command of the situation.

Lately she had seemed to defer to him, and frequently she used him as a sounding board about the work to be done at the farmhouse. It had struck him only the other day, quite forcibly, that she depended on him, and he was pleased about this. They had become good friends; he wished it could be more.

Tonight he had come over to discuss the detailed estimate for the electrical work at the farmhouse. He had given her a ballpark figure a week ago; then he had had to spend endless hours over at the farm, studying every aspect of the property inside and out. Now he was anxious to talk to her, get her approval of the figures.

From the doorway, Maggie said, 'Hello, Jake.'

He spun around, looked across at her. She was very pale. When she remained standing in the doorway, looking hesitant, he hurried across the room.

'Are you all right?' he asked quietly, drawing to a

standstill in front of her, his black eyebrows puckering together in a frown.

'I'll be fine in a minute,' Maggie answered. 'I'm afraid I became angry –' She broke off, biting her lip.

'Anything I can do to help?'

'No, thanks anyway.' Her voice was trembling and she paused again. Suddenly tears welled in her blue eyes and she looked at him helplessly.

'Maggie, what's wrong?' He could not bear to see the pain settling on her face. Concerned, he took a step towards her.

And as he did she moved towards him.

He reached for her, drew her to him, enfolded her in his arms.

'Maggie, Maggie, what is it? Please tell me what's bothering you?'

'I don't want to talk about it . . . I'll be all right in a . . . minute . . . really I will . . .'

But she wept on his shoulder, clinging to him fiercely.

He stroked her hair and kissed the top of her head, murmured gently, 'I'm here, I'll look after you. Please don't cry. I'm here for you.'

Turning suddenly, she twisted her face to stare up into his. Their eyes locked. He felt her trembling in his arms, and he tightened his grip on her.

Maggie's lips parted slightly, almost expectantly, and before he could stop himself he bent down and kissed her fully on the mouth.

She kissed him back, pressing her body against his. Because she was tall, almost as tall as he was, their bodies fitted together.

We're a perfect fit, Jake thought, his heart racing.

After a few moments of intense kissing, they stopped, drew apart, and stared at each other breathlessly, wonderingly.

Jake said softly, 'I've been wanting to do that for a long time.'

'I've been wanting you to do it,' Maggie whispered.

Emboldened, still staring hard at her, he went on, 'I've wanted to make love to you since that first night we met.'

'And I . . .'

'Oh Maggie, Maggie.'

'Jake.'

He drew her towards the sofa; they sank down onto it. Pushing her gently against the cushions, he leaned over her, looking deeply into her eyes. Bending closer, he kissed her eyelids, her nose, her face and lips, moved his mouth down into the hollow of her neck, then he began to unbutton her blouse. His hand slipped inside, cupped her breast; somehow he managed to release it from her bra.

When his mouth found her nipple, Maggie sighed deeply and moaned. And then she gave herself up to her feelings entirely, her hurt and pain of a short while ago forgotten for the moment.

She had thought of Jake constantly, had envisioned making love to him so often, she could scarcely believe it was happening now.

His mouth was soft if insistent, his touch gentle but firm, and when he stopped with suddenness she held herself perfectly still, wondering why he had stopped. She wanted him to continue.

A moment later his face was resting against her hair, and he said softly, 'Please, Maggie, let's go upstairs.'

'Yes,' she answered and he straightened, pulled her off the sofa; together they went up the wide staircase, their arms wrapped around each other.

Maggie pushed open her bedroom door, led him inside, and walked to the centre of the room.

Jake closed the door behind them and followed her.

The light outside was changing. The sky had turned a warm golden colour and it was flooding the room with a soft radiance.

He took hold of her shoulders and stared into her face. 'Be sure of this, Maggie.'

'I am, Jake.'

'Once this happens there's no going back. Not for me.'

'Nor me.'

He brought her into his arms.

They stood there for a long time, kissing, touching, familiarizing themselves with each other. They pulled apart, gazed at each other, started kissing again, their ardour growing.

Eventually, Jake began to undress her, taking off her blouse, unfastening her bra, then her skirt. Everything fell on the floor around her feet.

She stepped over the heap of clothes and stood gazing up at him intently, her emotions written all over her face: She wanted him.

Jake returned her gaze, recognized the need in her eyes and nodded slightly. He pulled his sweater over his head; Maggie stepped closer to him, began to unbutton his shirt, then took it off. He struggled out of his boots and jeans, and she took off her stockings and they came together totally naked.

They held each other tightly. Jake ran his strong hands over her shoulders, across her back and down onto her buttocks; she smoothed her hands over his shoulders, pushed them up into his thick hair.

Finally he led her over to the bed. After he had pressed her down onto it, he bent forward, kissed her, then said, 'I'll only be a minute.'

Maggie lay waiting for him, her heart beating rapidly. It was years and years since she had felt like this, had wanted a man so much. She wished he would hurry, come back. She could hardly wait.

Jake walked across the room towards the bed.

She thought he looked magnificent.

He stood next to the bed, staring down at her. He noticed that her eyes had turned the darkest of blues, so dark they were almost purple, the dark bluish-purple of pansies. They were full of urgent desire for him, he recognized that once more and he felt heat rising in him, his excitement growing as he stood looking at her.

How beautiful she was in her nakedness, in the soft golden radiance of the fading light, he thought. He had not realized what a lovely body she had, covered as it always was with her bulky sweaters and heavy jackets and long, flowing skirts.

But she was very slim, he noted, with curving hips, and long, long legs. She had perfect breasts, softly rounded, and her skin was smooth and pale.

As Maggie returned his long, contemplative gaze

she thought that a man's body could be beautiful. His was. Jake was tall and slim; he had a broad chest and wide shoulders above slender hips and long legs. He was splendid to look at. She could hardly tear her eyes away.

Jake joined her on the bed at last.

He took her in his arms and held her close to him, kissing her hair and her neck, smoothing his hands over her marvellous breasts. He began to kiss her mouth.

Maggie kissed him back ardently. Their kisses grew hot, harder and hotter still, more passionate than before.

Jake propped himself up on one elbow, looked into her face and traced his finger along the line of her mouth. 'I want you so much,' he murmured. 'But I don't want us to hurry. I want to prolong this, savour it.' He bent into her. 'You really excite me, Maggie; if we're not careful it'll be over all too quickly.'

She half smiled, said nothing.

He went on quietly, 'I've wanted this for so long, ached to be with you.'

'I felt the same.' She paused, eyed him carefully. 'But I thought you weren't interested in me.'

'I thought the same . . . of you.'

Reaching up, she touched his face lightly with her fingertips. 'We're a couple of fools.' She ran a finger around his mouth, thinking how sensual it was.

He took hold of her hand, put her finger in his mouth and began sucking it, curling his tongue around it. Maggie felt the heat surging through her, settling in her loins. He was exciting her . . . there was something so erotic about the way he was sucking. She felt herself growing moist.

After a moment he stopped and said, in a voice thickened by emotion, 'I love you, Maggie. I want you to hear this now. Not in the heat of it all, when I might well say it. I want you to know it's true, not just the sex talking.'

Startled, she simply nodded.

Putting her arms around his neck, she drew his face down to hers. She kissed him deeply, as he did her. Their mouths locked together, their tongues entwining. Maggie felt as though he were sucking the breath out of her, and she grew more excited than ever. Desire flooded her, blinded her to everything except him.

Abruptly Jake moved his head, began to kiss her breasts, cupping them together in both of his hands, moving his mouth from one nipple to the other, brushing his lips over them until they stood erect in the centre of their dark, plum-coloured aureoles.

Moving on, thrilling to her, tremendously aroused now, Jake trailed his mouth down over her stomach, and his hands followed, smoothing and stroking.

Jake lifted his head, looked at her face. Her eyes were closed. 'Maggie,' he said softly.

'Yes?'

'Am I pleasing you? Can I love you this way?'

'Oh yes.'

He began to make love to her tenderly, wanting to give her pleasure. He touched the core of her lightly at first, but as his supple fingers began to know her they became more insistent. He explored and massaged the flower of her womanhood, did so expertly, tantalizingly, enjoying touching her in this most intimate way, feeling her coming alive under his hands.

Maggie lay very still, hardly breathing. Her longing for him was rampant; her body ached to be joined to his. She felt herself opening up to him more and more as his mouth followed where his fingers had been. He lavished her with kisses and his tongue was a darting arrow hitting its mark. She began to pulse under his kisses.

And then suddenly she was spiralling up into ecstasy as wave after wave of pleasure rolled over her. She convulsed, her body arching slightly as he brought her to a climax; and she cried out his name harshly.

Jake moved his body onto hers, parting her legs wider with his own. He had an enormous erection but she was ready for him, and he slid right into her, thrusting deeply.

Maggie was panting, moving against him, matching his rhythm, floating with him somewhere she had never been before.

Higher and higher she rose as he moved deeper and deeper into her, and once again the waves of ecstasy started, began to engulf her.

Jake knew he was touching the core of her with the core of himself. He was strong and hard inside her, riding the crest of her second climax with her. This was the way it was meant to be. The way it should always be and never had been for him. Until her.

She was cresting higher and higher, flying into the

unknown, saying his name over and over.

He let himself go, crested with her, gave himself up to her, flowed with her and into her. And he shouted out, 'Oh Maggie! Oh my love!'

The colours of the sky had changed again, the bright golden radiance laced through with crimson, magenta and violet. It was that magic hour, twilight, just before darkness falls, when everything looks soft and rosy and at peace.

Jake lay on top of Maggie, his head between her breasts. Her hands rested lightly on his shoulders. After a while she began to stroke his back and then his hair.

His voice was muffled when he said, 'I don't ever want to move. I want to stay right here forever.'

Maggie said nothing. She bent over him and kissed the top of his head, thinking of his words earlier, before their passionate lovemaking. He had told her he loved her, startling her with this declaration. But she believed him. Jake always meant what he said and he was very sincere. She felt the same way about him, but for days now she had been suppressing her feelings, convinced he had no interest in her. How wrong she had been. But nothing could ever come of this, there was too big a difference in their ages.

Before she could stop herself, Maggie said, 'I'm a lot older than you, Jake.'

'I like older women,' he laughed. 'They're more interesting.' He chuckled again. 'Anyway, you don't look it.'

'But I am. I'm almost forty-four.'

'Numbers don't mean anything. And I told you, you don't look much older than thirty-two, thirty-three. But who cares?'

'I do. How old are you?'

'How old do you think I am?' he asked in a teasing voice.

'Thirty, thirty-one.'

'Wrong. Guess again.'

'I can't. Please tell me.'

'I'll be sixteen in June.'

'Be serious, Jake!'

He laughed. 'Okay, okay. I'm twenty-eight until June the twelfth. Then I'll be twenty-nine.'

'That makes me fifteen years –'

'Who's counting!' he exclaimed peremptorily, cutting her off. He lifted himself up, lay next to her, taking her in his arms.

Jake started kissing her, quietly at first and then more passionately, and soon he was moving on top of her. He was fully aroused and he entered her quickly, without preamble, possessing her more forcibly than before.

'Oh God, how I want you,' he groaned against her hair. 'I've never wanted a woman the way I want you, Maggie. I want all of you, every bit of you. Come to me, please come to me.'

'Oh Jake,' she cried, 'I want you too, you must know that.'

He pushed his hands under her buttocks, brought her even closer to him. They moved together with rhythmic grace, rising and falling as one. They soared, crested on the heat of their passion for each other.

Finally they lay still, their breathing rapid and harsh.

When Jake regained his breath he said against her neck, 'And you think age matters ... this is what counts. This ... this ... chemistry between us, Maggie. It doesn't often happen, at least not like this, with such intensity. It's very rare ...'

When she was silent, he said, 'You do know that, don't you?'

'Yes.'

'What we have together is something very powerful, and believe me, age has nothing to do with it.'

They ate supper together in the kitchen. It was a simple meal which Maggie had prepared quickly: scrambled eggs, English muffins and coffee.

'More like breakfast, I'm afraid,' Maggie said, smiling across the table at him. 'I haven't had a chance to do much shopping this week.'

'I don't mind. I was starving.' Jake smiled back at her and added, 'Can I have it again for breakfast, please? You are going to let me spend the night, aren't you?'

'If you want to,' she replied, and felt suddenly shy with him.

'I want.' He reached out and took hold of her hand and squeezed it. Then he lifted it to his lips and kissed her fingers. 'You have beautiful hands, Maggie, such long, supple fingers. And *you're* beautiful.' He shook his head. 'Oh God, you do have a terrible effect on me ... I could take you back to bed right now and do it all over again.'

As he finished speaking he began to kiss the tips of her fingers, her knuckles and the spaces in between. Then he turned her hand over and kissed the palm. After a second he lifted his eyes and looked at her. 'Don't ever doubt this, Maggie. It's real and it's the best.'

She stared back. His face was serious, his light green eyes intense, and there was so much yearning for her in them she was touched. She felt herself choking up for a reason she couldn't fathom. 'Oh Jake,' was all she could say, and for a split second she thought she was going to weep.

As if sensing this, and wishing to avert it, Jake rose and said, 'How about some more coffee?'

She shook her head. 'No, thanks.'

He went and filled his own cup, returned to the table, and sat down opposite her once more.

There was a small silence between them. It was broken by Jake, who said in a low voice, 'You were very upset earlier, Maggie.'

'Yes, I was,' she agreed. Giving him a candid look, she continued, 'I think I should explain something.'

'If you like, but it's up to you. I don't want to pry.'

'A few weeks ago Samantha made a reference to my divorce. So I know you know I was married once. You do, don't you?'

'Yes, I'd gathered that.'

'What you don't know is that I have two children. Twins. A boy and a girl. They'll be twenty-one in a couple of weeks. They live in Chicago. They're attending Northwestern. Anyway, I had hoped we could all be together for their birthday, but their father is taking them away for a long weekend in California. Without me. When you arrived earlier this evening I was talking to my daughter Hannah, who was explaining this to me. Naturally, I was very upset to be excluded.'

'I don't blame you. That's kind of a lousy thing to do, isn't it?' He raised a brow quizzically, then rushed to add, 'In my opinion it is.'

'I agree.' Maggie shook her head. 'But it's par for the course.'

'What do you mean?'

She sighed. 'You've never been married, never had children, Jake, so it would be hard for you to understand all the ramifications. In any case, I prefer not to talk about it anymore. I just wanted you to know I was upset about something personal and not business.'

He nodded and changed the subject.

CHAPTER
8

T HE JANGLING TELEPHONE brought
Maggie out of the shower swiftly. Grabbing a large
bath towel, she wrapped it around herself and raced
through into her bedroom.

Reaching for the phone, she said, 'Hello?'

'It's me.'

'Hello, Jake!' she exclaimed, as always delighted to
hear his voice. 'We're still on for ten o'clock, aren't
we?'

'You bet,' he answered quickly. 'The only thing is,
I'd like to meet you a bit earlier. Is that possible?'

'Of course, Jake, but is there something wrong?'

There was the merest hesitation before he said in a
rather tentative voice, 'No, not really, Maggie. I just
want to talk to you about something, that's all.'

'What? You sound odd. Tell me now, Jake, tell me on the phone.'

'I prefer to talk to you in person, Maggie, face to face. Really I do.'

There was something in his voice that alarmed her, but knowing him the way she did she knew he would not succumb to pressure from her. She said, 'All right then. What time do you want to meet?'

'Nine-thirty. If that's okay with you?'

'It's fine. Do you want to come here?'

'No. I'll meet you at the site,' he answered swiftly.

'All right.'

'See you then.'

' 'Bye, Jake.'

Maggie stood with her hand resting on the phone, a puzzled look on her face. His voice had been peculiar and so had his words and his delivery. He had been almost, but not quite, abrupt with her. This was unlike him. Also, she had detected a nervousness in him, and she could not help thinking he was about to break off with her. What else could it be?

She sat down heavily on the bed, shivering suddenly, even though it was a lovely May morning, warm and sunny outside. Her heart sank. Yes, that was it. He was going to end their relationship. Sighing, she lay back on the pillows and closed her eyes, thinking of Jake Cantrell. It was exactly a week ago today that they had first made love here in this bed.

Crazy, exciting, passionate love. He had been insatiable, unable to get enough of her, bringing her back to bed after they had eaten her potluck supper of scrambled eggs. And she had felt the same way; desire had overwhelmed her.

It seemed to Maggie that they hadn't stopped making love since then, although this was not strictly true. They had managed to do an enormous amount of work together at the farmhouse, or the site, as he called it.

But, now that she looked back, he had been odd for the last couple of days, withdrawn and shy with her. It suddenly struck her that his demeanour had been the same as it had on the first night they had met with Samantha to discuss *The Crucible*.

Opening her eyes, Maggie resolutely pushed herself up and left the bed. She went back to the bathroom, finished her toilet, and then returned to the bedroom to dress for the working day ahead.

Since it was warm and sunny, she chose a pair of lightweight navy blue gabardine trousers with a matching jacket and took out a white cotton T-shirt. Once she was dressed, she hurried downstairs to her office and put her papers in her briefcase.

A few minutes later, just before nine, she left the house, knowing it would take her a good half hour to drive to the farm near Bull's Bridge Corner in South Kent.

Jake's pick-up truck was already parked outside the old red barn when she arrived. Bringing her Jeep to a standstill, Maggie alighted, picked up her briefcase and slammed the door.

As she went into the farmhouse, heading for the kitchen, she braced herself, not knowing what he was going to say to her, not knowing what to expect.

He stood up when he saw her and smiled faintly, almost apologetically, but he made no move in her direction, as he would normally have done.

Maggie thought he looked drawn, on edge, and his light green eyes, usually so full of vitality and life, were dull and anxious.

'Hi,' Maggie said from the doorway.

He nodded. 'Thanks for coming early. I wanted a chance to talk to you before the other guys arrived. Come and sit here at the table, Maggie. I brought a Thermos of iced tea. Would you like some?'

She shrugged, then walked into the room briskly. 'Why not?' Sitting down at the table she waited for him to pour the tea, thanked him and said, 'Why didn't you want to talk to me on the phone, Jake? What's this all about?' Maggie heard the strain and anxiety in her voice and she was annoyed with herself.

Jake cleared his throat several times, and explained, 'I've been feeling terrible this past week, Maggie, really awful. Ever since we made love last Wednesday.' He cleared his throat again. 'I . . . I . . . look, I just haven't been fair to you.'

Staring hard at him, she asked, 'What do you mean, Jake?'

He shook his head, and looked embarrassed when he said in a sudden rush of words, 'I haven't been exactly honest with you. It's not that I've lied to you, because I haven't, but there's something I should have told you. And I guess I've had a very guilty conscience. I just couldn't stand it any longer. That's why I wanted to see you this morning. *Explain.*'

'What is it, Jake?' Maggie asked, sounding slightly perplexed. 'What are you trying to say to me?'

'Last Wednesday night you made a remark about me not understanding why you were upset because I'd never been married, never had children. But I have been married, Maggie, and I should have told you so then. I didn't though, and I lied by omission. It's been troubling me.'

Maggie sat back in the chair, her large blue eyes riveted on him. 'Are you a married man cheating on his wife? Is that what you're trying to tell me?'

Colour suffused his face and he exclaimed vehemently, 'No! I'm not! I've been separated for over a year. I'm in the middle of a divorce. I live alone and I rarely ever see Amy. And I hope to be single again soon. But look, I should have told you before. I'm sorry,' he finished quietly.

She heard the misery in his voice, saw the contrite expression on his handsome face, and reached out and took hold of his hand. 'It's all right, Jake, really it is.'

'You're not mad at me?'

Maggie shook her head and smiled at him. 'Of course not. Anyway, I don't get mad that easily. It has to be something really important to get me going . . . like my children's defection, for example.'

Jake said, 'You didn't explain that to me . . . I'm not sure I understand what's going on.'

Taking a deep breath, Maggie said, 'We've never had a proper talk, you and I, Jake. We were friends involved in a drama group, and then we started to work together professionally, when suddenly, unexpectedly, we became lovers. We don't know very much about each other. Let me tell you about me. Okay?'

'Yes, I want to know all about you, Maggie.'

She chuckled. 'I'm not so sure I'm going to tell you *everything*. I think I should remain a little mysterious, don't you?'

He laughed with her and nodded.

'Two years ago my husband left me for a younger woman. Mike Sorrell's a very successful lawyer in Chicago, and he dumped me for a twenty-seven-year-old lawyer he'd met and was working with on a case. I ought to have known something like that was going to happen, things hadn't been right between us for a very long time. But what threw me, truly hurt me, was my children's defection. I've never really been able to understand why they took Mike's side when he was the guilty party.' Maggie gave Jake a long, thoughtful look, and added softly, 'Except that he's the one with all the money, of course.'

'Little shits,' Jake said, and then flushing slightly, he murmured, 'Sorry, I shouldn't be making remarks like that.'

'It's okay, Jake, I understand, and I've often thought the same thing. Anyway, I wanted them to celebrate their twenty-first birthday with me, and I had written to Hannah, some weeks ago actually. When I didn't hear from her, I phoned her. You came in on the tail end of my conversation. The upshot is that she and her twin brother Peter are going to spend their birthday with their father. He's taking them to some beautiful inn in Sonoma for the weekend.'

'And you're not invited.'

'No.'

'I'm sorry, Maggie, really sorry they're hurting you in this way. I wish I could make it up to you.'

'Thanks, Jake,' she said, squeezing his hand. 'But I'm better now, I'm over it. Well, more or less.' Maggie sighed and said in a low voice, 'In a way, I think I'd written them off . . . they haven't shown much interest in me ever since all this happened.' Forcing a laugh, she added, 'I guess I wasn't a very good mother.'

'Knowing what I know about you, I bet you were a hell of a mother!' Jake exclaimed. 'And kids in this kind of situation can be very . . . treacherous. I think that's the best word. I know my sister Patty is going through something similar. She got married a couple of years ago. Her husband was a divorced man, and his children have been behaving very badly lately. Not only towards him but Patty as well. And she had nothing to do with their parents' divorce. Bill had been single for four years when she met him. Things were apparently relatively okay between him and his kids until he married Patty. Then they turned nasty and adopted a very hostile stance.' Jake shook his head. 'God knows why.'

'You said you were separated, Jake. Do you have children?'

'No, I don't. Sadly. Well, perhaps I shouldn't say that now that we're getting divorced. I wanted children, though. Amy didn't.'

'I see,' Maggie murmured, looking at him through thoughtful eyes, then she said, 'You must have been married very young.'

'Nineteen. We were both nineteen. We'd been friends since we were twelve, sort of childhood sweethearts in high school.'

'I married young, too, just after I left Bennington College, when I was twenty-two. I had the twins a year later.'

'And you were living in Chicago all those years?'

'Yes, that's Mike's home town. I come from New York, I grew up in Manhattan. Where are you from, Jake? Kent?'

'No, Hartford. I was born there. After Amy and I were married we lived there for a while, then we moved to New Milford. Once we separated last year I lived in a studio apartment on Bank Street. Until I found the house on Route 341, that is.'

'Where does Amy live now?'

'She's still in New Milford.' Jake took a long swallow of his iced tea and went on, 'Do you know Samantha from New York? From when you were growing up, I mean?'

'No, we met at Bennington. And we became instant friends. Best friends.' Maggie smiled as she thought of Samantha with affection. 'I don't know what I would have done without her. Especially in the last couple of years. I don't think I would have managed to survive without her.'

'Oh yes you would,' Jake remarked in a knowing voice. 'You're a born survivor. That's one of the things I admire about you, Maggie. Your strength of character, your resilience. You're a very special woman. I've never met anyone like you.'

'Thank you. I've never met anyone quite like you, Jake.'

He stared at her.

She stared back.

Jake said softly, 'You do care about me then?'

'Oh yes, I do,' she answered.

'Is everything all right between us?'

She nodded, smiled.

He also smiled, relief flooding his eyes. 'I couldn't stand it if you were angry with me.'

Suddenly Maggie laughed, feeling relieved herself. 'I feel the same way.'

'Can I see you tonight?'

'I'd love it.'

'Would you like to come to my house? I could make pasta and a salad. I'd like to go over the final lighting designs for *The Crucible* with you.'

'That's a good idea! I'd like to show you my drawings for the sets and finalize everything with you. There's not much time left, especially since Samantha and I are going away.'

'Oh. When is that?' he asked swiftly, sounding surprised.

'In about six weeks. In July.'

'Where are you going?'

'To Scotland. And then we're stopping off in London for a few days, on our way home. The trip's been planned for a long time. It's partly business.'

'I'll miss you,' Jake said. But he didn't really know how much until she had gone.

CHAPTER
9

IN HIS WHOLE LIFE Jake had never missed anyone the way he missed Maggie Sorrell. She had only been gone five days, but to him it seemed like five months.

It would be another ten days before she returned to Kent, and he knew he was going to be miserable until then. He was glad they were involved professionally as well as personally, working on the remodelling of Havers Hill. It made him feel closer to her, especially when he went to the old farmhouse. Her presence was everywhere.

For the same reason, he'd been up to the Little Theatre in Kent twice, to tinker around with the lighting for the play, and he planned to go there again before she returned.

The woman designing the costumes, Alice Ferrier, was a friend of Samantha's and Maggie's, and he enjoyed chatting to her, and to the stagehands working on Maggie's sets. It gave him a sense of belonging to Maggie's group, was like being part of a large family, and he enjoyed the camaraderie. Also, it helped to deflect the loneliness he was feeling in her absence.

Until he met Maggie, Jake had been self-sufficient, going about his business, doing his own thing, occasionally seeing the odd male friend, and he'd had a couple of short-lived affairs. But he had never relied on anyone for anything.

Now he felt that Maggie was necessary to his well-being, his very existence, and this bothered him. He disliked being dependent on another human being; it made him feel vulnerable.

At the outset of their relationship, the night they had slept together for the first time, Jake had come right out and said it – told Maggie that he loved her. It was true, he did.

But Maggie had not declared herself. He was not really worried, although he would like to hear her say it, because he knew she cared about him. Cared a lot. She gave herself away constantly.

Thoughts of Maggie continued to swirl in his head as he went out of the kitchen and crossed the yard, heading for the old red barn in the field at the back of the house. He had turned it into a studio and workshop, and he wanted to complete the plans he was drawing up for the exterior lighting at Havers Hill Farm. He wished Maggie had been with him at the farm today; finally he had come up with solutions for some of the more intricate lighting problems and he would have enjoyed explaining them to her.

Jake paused as he walked down the path, staring at an unusual brown-coloured bird with an orange breast that had just flown out of the giant oak which shaded the lawn. As the bird hopped along at the edge of the grass he wondered what species it was. He had never seen this kind of bird before. The garden and fields surrounding his house were full of wildlife, as were the wetlands that stretched beyond. Canada geese and ducks made the wetlands their habitat.

Wandering on towards the barn, he stopped again as a chipmunk skittered across his path and disappeared into the innards of an old stone wall; the entire place was a haven for these funny little creatures and squirrels and rabbits. A fleeting thought crossed his mind – that this place would be a natural wonderland for a child.

As Jake struggled with the lock on the door, which was stuck, he could hear the phone ringing inside, but by the time he managed to get the door opened it had stopped.

Could it have been Maggie phoning from Scotland? he wondered. He hoped so; she had said she would give him a call this week. He depressed the button on the answering machine.

'It's me, Jake,' he heard Amy's voice saying. 'I've got to talk to you. It's urgent. Please call me.'

Immediately he dialled her apartment. The phone rang and rang. There was no answer. Just as there had been no answer yesterday, even though he had received the same kind of message on his machine last night. Obviously she wanted to talk to him about something, but when he returned her calls she was not there.

Walking over to the long table which served as a desk for him, he resolved to buy her an answering machine. Since she hadn't bothered to get one, as he had suggested months ago, he was going to have to do it for her.

Jake sighed under his breath. That was the story of his life with Amy. For as long as he could remember, ever since they were twelve, he had always been the one to take care of everything, and he had always had to look after her. She was like a baby. She couldn't manage to do the simplest task. Eventually it had begun to irritate him.

The odd thing was he *wanted* to take care of Maggie, to look after *her*, even though there was no need. She was such a competent woman and well able to take care of herself. Over the last few months he had come to know her well, and he was aware that she was clever and practical, but he still felt the need to protect her. Certainly he saw a vulnerability in her, a softness he found most appealing.

Pushing aside thoughts of Maggie and Amy, Jake turned on the architect's lamp he used on the old oak table, pulled a drawing pad towards him and began making sketches for the exterior lighting systems at Havers Hill Farm.

The red barn where he was working had become a refuge for him since he had moved into the house. He found the big open space conducive to work, whether it was designing lighting effects, tinkering with lamps and other electrical equipment at the bench, or painting at the easel under the big window situated at the far end of the barn. These three areas were quite separate and self-contained, and he had furnished the barn sparsely. It was austere, painted white, and only the things required for his work had been used. His one luxury was a CD player, so that he could listen to music whenever he felt like it.

Jake concentrated on the plans for lighting the trees at Havers Hill for an hour, and then he tried Amy's number again. There was still no answer, and immediately he turned his attention back to the plans in front of him. He had always had tunnel vision, and this had served him well.

At nine he stopped working, shut off the lights, left the barn and went back to the house. He found a cold beer in the refrigerator, made himself a cheese-and-tomato sandwich and took his evening snack into the living room. After turning on the television, he sat down in the chair, ate his sandwich, drank his beer and absentmindedly channel surfed. He was preoccupied with thoughts of Maggie, missing her, wanting her, longing to see her.

When the phone rang again Jake jumped up, grabbed it and exclaimed, 'Hello?' hoping it was she.

'It's me,' Amy said. 'I've been trying to get you for two days. Why haven't you called me back, Jake?'

'I have, Amy,' he answered, striving not to sound impatient. 'I got your message when I came home from work last night. I phoned you. No answer. I

117

tried you at the store this morning and was told it was your day off. I just missed your call by a few seconds tonight. You must have gone out immediately, because there was no answer and I dialled you within minutes.'

'I went to the movies with Mavis.'

'I see.' He cleared his throat. 'You said you wanted to talk to me urgently. What about?'

'Something important.'

'Then tell me, Amy, I'm listening,' he said, sitting down on the arm of the sofa. When there was no response from her, he said in an even tone, 'Come on, Amy, tell me what this is about.'

'Not on the phone. I need to talk to you in person. Can't you come over?'

'*Now?*'

'Yes, Jake.'

'Amy, I can't! It's too late! It's turned ten, and I have to be up very early. Let's talk now if it's so important to you.'

'*No!* I have to *see* you.'

'Well, I'm not driving over to New Milford at this hour, so you can forget that!'

'Can I see you tomorrow? It's really urgent that we meet.'

'All right,' he agreed, although he did so reluctantly.

'Tomorrow night, Jake? I could make you supper.'

'No, no, that's not necessary,' he replied and, thinking swiftly, he improvised, 'I have to go to New Milford tomorrow morning to pick up some

118

equipment. I need it for the job I'm doing in South Kent. How about if I come to the store around noon? I'll take you to lunch.'

'I guess so . . . I wish you could come over now . . .'

'I'll see you tomorrow,' he said firmly. 'Good night, Amy.'

' 'Bye, Jake,' she muttered and hung up.

Later, as he undressed, Jake asked himself if he had made a mistake, agreeing to see Amy. There was no question in his mind that she was going to grumble about the divorce, try to talk him out of it. She was already procrastinating; there had been no word from her lawyer. He wasn't even sure she had been to see him again. He was going to have to do something about it himself, take matters into his own hands, he decided, if he ever wanted to be free. As usual, Amy was incapable of handling it.

When they met the following day, the first thing Jake noticed about Amy was that she had made an effort with her appearance. Her wispy blonde hair was pulled back in a ponytail and tied with a blue ribbon, and she had applied a little make-up.

Nevertheless, as he sat looking at her across the table in the Wayfarers Café in New Milford, where he had brought her for lunch, he thought she looked tired. She was only twenty-eight, but it struck him now that she appeared older, a little worn down. But this was nothing new, really; there had been something lacklustre about her for the past few years. Amy had faded quickly. It saddened him really, and he couldn't help feeling a little bit sorry for her. She wasn't a bad person, just unfocused, disorganized and isolated.

They chatted about inconsequential things, looked at the menus, discussed what they would like to eat. In the end they both settled on the Cobb salad and iced tea.

Once the waitress had taken their order and they were alone, Amy said, 'So what's the job you're doing in Kent?'

'A farmhouse,' he explained. 'A very old place, actually. It's picturesque and has beautiful grounds. It's a challenge, especially the interiors. I'm also doing the outside, creating lighting for the landscaped areas and the pool. It's a big job for me and I'm pretty excited about it.'

She nodded. 'I know you like doing intricate work, the fancy stuff, and you're good at it, Jake.'

'Thanks.' He gave her an appraising glance and said, 'What is it you want to talk to me about, Amy?'

'Let's wait until after lunch.'

'*Why?* You've been calling me for two days, asking me to meet you, saying it's urgent, and now you want to wait.'

She nodded. Her mouth settled in a stubborn line.

Jake let out a small sigh. 'Whatever you say, Amy, but I do have to go back to work you know. In a couple of hours.'

'My mother doesn't think we should get a divorce,' she blurted out, and then took a quick sip of water, eyeing him over the rim of the glass.

'I know that,' he replied, his eyes narrowing slightly. 'Is that why you wanted to see me? To discuss the divorce? Has your mother been going on at you?'

She shook her head. 'Not really.'

Jake leaned forward over the table and pinned her with his eyes. 'Look, Amy, I'm sorry it didn't work out, really sorry. But there it is ... these things happen, you know that.'

Before she could answer the waitress was back, placing the salads in front of them, returning a second later with the glasses of iced tea.

They ate in silence for a while. Or rather Jake ate; Amy picked at her food.

Finally she put down her fork and leaned back in the chair.

Jake glanced at her, frowning slightly. Suddenly she looked pale, paler than usual, he thought, and she seemed to be on the verge of tears.

'What is it, Amy? What's wrong?' he asked, putting his fork on the plate. When she didn't answer, but gaped at him oddly, looking scared, he pressed, 'What's the matter, honey?'

'I'm sick,' she began and stopped with abruptness.

His frown intensified. 'I'm not following you. Do you mean you feel nauseous at this moment? Or are you saying you have an illness?'

'Yes. I went to the doctor, Jake. I haven't been feeling well.' Her eyes brimmed. 'It's cancer. He told me I've got ovarian cancer.'

'Oh my God! Amy! No! Is he sure?' Jake leaned forward and took her hand, holding it tightly in his. 'Is the doctor certain?'

'Oh yes,' she whispered.

For a moment Jake was at a loss for words. A compassionate man by nature, he filled with sympathy for her. He wondered how he could comfort her, and then realized there was no way. His words, if he could find the right ones, would be cold comfort. Far better to leave them unsaid. And so he sat there, holding her hand, patting it from time to time, hoping he was making her feel less alone.

CHAPTER
10

It HAD RAINED EARLIER, and as Maggie walked down the path that led through the garden of Sunlaws House Hotel she paused for a moment and lifted her eyes to the sky. The sun was coming out again, penetrating the light clouds, and quite suddenly a rainbow trembled up there above the trees, a perfect arc of pink and blue, violet and yellow.

Maggie smiled inwardly, thinking it was a good omen. Her mother had been the most positive person she had ever known, one who had always believed in the pot of gold at the end of the rainbow, silver linings and bluebirds bringing happiness.

Mom was an eternal optimist, she thought, still smiling to herself, filled with the fondest of memories. I'm glad I inherited that trait from her. If I hadn't I don't think I would have survived the debacle with Mike Sorrell. They would have taken me away in a straitjacket. But she had indeed survived and life had never been better for her, she decided. And then she thought: how many people get a second chance at life?

When she reached the end of the path, Maggie turned around and headed back to the hotel. She and Samantha were staying here overnight, en route to London by rented car. They had driven down from Edinburgh and Glasgow, and had arrived at Sunlaws in time for lunch.

The manor was in Kelso, in the area known as The Borders, in the heart of Roxburghshire. The gracious old house, which belonged to the Duke and Duchess of Roxburghe, had been turned into the most charming of country hotels.

Sunlaws was handsomely furnished, full of mellow antiques and fine paintings, and it was imbued with the comfort and welcoming warmth that Maggie loved. It was a look and an environment that she strove hard to create in her own decorating schemes for her clients.

The landscape around the hotel was equally captivating, and it reminded her of the northwestern highlands of Connecticut. The moment she had set eyes on it she had begun to feel homesick.

Maggie now realized that she couldn't wait to get back to her house in Kent. And to Jake. He was constantly on her mind; she rarely stopped thinking about him, wishing he were here, wishing he could be sharing this trip with her. And she wished he had been with her when she bought the antiques in Edinburgh and Glasgow. They were for the farmhouse and were good pieces made of dark, ripe wood, some of them handcarved, and all were very old and beautifully made. They would sit perfectly in the rooms at Havers Hill Farm, would underscore the mood of the house and its overall feeling of antiquity.

Maggie was glad she had come to Scotland with Samantha. The trip had been highly successful for both of them. Apart from the antique furniture she had purchased, she had found other interesting things: antique lamps, porcelains and all sorts of unique accessories.

Samantha had invested in a variety of fabrics which she planned to sell in the studio shop she was opening in three months' time. Maggie's favourites were the Scottish wools, mohairs and tartans, which had taken her fancy as well as Samantha's.

All in all they had done well, and Maggie made up her mind to come back next year. With Jake. He had never travelled abroad and had recently confided that he would enjoy making a trip to England one day.

She had missed him, missed his warmth and affection, his sense of fun, his dry humour, his passion, and his constant cosseting of her. He made her feel so wanted, so loved, in a way which Mike Sorrell never had.

She heard her name and glanced up, peering ahead, shading her eyes against the bright light with her hand. She waved when she saw Samantha coming down the path towards her.

'I've been looking all over for you!' Samantha

exclaimed, tucking her arm through Maggie's, falling into step. The two of them continued on to the hotel together.

Maggie said, 'I love this time of day, just before dark. It's magic.'

Samantha nodded. 'So do I. And that's what they call it in the movie business . . . *the magic hour*. Apparently cinematographers think it's the most wonderful light for filming.' Samantha shivered. 'Let's go inside, Maggie, it's turned coolish. There's a breeze blowing up for one thing, and it smells of rain.'

'I'm a bit cold myself,' Maggie admitted.

They increased their pace, and once they were inside the hotel Samantha looked at her watch. She said, 'It's nearly seven. Let's go and have a drink in the lounge. There's a huge fire blazing in there. It might be July, but they know something about these cool Scottish nights, the locals do.'

A short while later the two friends sat in the comfortable lounge. It was furnished with deep leather chairs and sofas, and there were wonderful old paintings on the walls. Vases of flowers were everywhere and their mingled scents filled the air. The only sounds were the ticking of a clock somewhere at the other end of the room and the hiss and crackle of the logs burning in the huge marble fireplace. Silk-shaded lamps had been turned on and the lounge had a soft glow to it.

Samantha looked around and said, 'It's so intimate and cosy in here, and the room has a real country-house feeling to it, don't you think?'

'It's a look that's hard to reproduce properly,' Maggie said. 'The British do it so well, maybe because it's endemic to their way of life.'

Samantha merely smiled and took a sip of her white wine. Then she glanced across at Maggie. 'I've really enjoyed the trip, haven't you?'

'Yes, I have.'

Now Samantha eyed her carefully and murmured, 'But you've missed Jake, haven't you?'

Maggie smiled. 'A bit . . .' She laughed, added, 'A lot actually. How did you guess?'

'You've seemed distracted sometimes, and sort of . . . well, *faraway* is the best way of describing it.'

Maggie was silent. She averted her face for a brief moment, sat gazing into the fire, a quiet, reflective expression settling in her eyes. After a moment she glanced at her best friend and said, 'There's something I want to tell you.'

Samantha nodded. 'And oddly enough, I've got something to tell you. But you go first.'

There was a fractional silence. Maggie then said, 'I'm pregnant, Sam.'

'Good God! You can't be! Surely not! Not in this day and age! Don't tell me you didn't use anything, for God's sake!'

'Yes. I missed my period for the second time last week, when we first got here. And no, we didn't use anything.'

Samantha sat back, gaping at her askance. 'There's something out there called AIDS, Maggie.'

'I know. But . . . well . . . I trust Jake, I know he's not promiscuous.'

129

'When you slept with Jake you slept with everybody else he's ever been with ... you don't know anything about *them*.'

Maggie did not respond. She leaned back against the tapestry cushions in the leather chair and stared into space. Then finally rousing herself, she muttered, 'You said you had something to tell me. What is it?'

Samantha hesitated, cleared her throat, and leaning closer to Maggie, she said quietly, 'You'd better know this, even though it might hurt more than ever. Jake's a married man, Mag. I found out just before we left, but I didn't want to tell you then and upset you. However, I thought you should know, now that we're heading back home. I purposely waited so as not to spoil your trip.'

Maggie said quickly, 'But I already know that! He told me himself, weeks ago. Actually, it was a few days after we became lovers. He was very honest with me, Sam. He said he had been separated for a year, living alone for that time, and was in the middle of a divorce. Are you suggesting he's still living with his wife?'

Samantha shook her head and said swiftly, 'No, no, I'm not.'

'Who told you he was married?'

'A client. She bought me a present from the bath and body shop in New Milford. When she gave the basket of goodies to me, all kinds of aromatherapy products, she said they'd been recommended by Amy Cantrell. I suppose I must have reacted to the name, and my client said something about Amy being the wife of Jake Cantrell, the lighting expert. But if you say he's separated, then I'm sure he is.'

'And he does live alone,' Maggie asserted. 'I've been to his house several times.'

'Why didn't you tell me he was in the middle of a divorce?'

Maggie shrugged. 'I didn't think it was particularly important, Sam.'

'What are you going to do about the baby, Maggie?'

'I'm going to have it, of course.'

Samantha gave her a questioning stare. 'What about Jake? I mean, what do you think he'll say? Do?'

'I'm sure he'll be pleased. I hope so. But in any case it's my choice, and only mine. I'm certainly not going to have an abortion.'

Maggie leaned forward, and her face was suddenly bright with happiness and hope, when she added, 'While I was walking in the garden earlier, I couldn't help thinking that not many people get a second chance in life. I *did*. The baby's my second chance, and Jake of course. I think I'm very lucky.'

'Do you think he'll want to marry you?'

'I don't know ... I don't really care ... about making it legal. I can bring up a baby myself and support a child. I'm very competent, Sam.'

'You don't have to tell me! I know that only too well,' Samantha remarked pithily.

'Maybe you think I'm crazy,' Maggie ventured. 'Here I am, forty-four years old, pregnant by my much younger lover of twenty-nine, who's not even divorced yet, whom I'm not sure even wants to marry me.' She began to laugh and lifted her hands in a

131

helpless gesture. 'And do I want to marry him?' Maggie shrugged and lifted a dark brow.

Samantha shook her head wonderingly. 'There's nobody like you, Maggie, when it comes to coping. Let's not forget that you came through a pretty rotten situation with your husband of twenty-odd years who decided to take a walk. A situation which might have felled many another woman.'

'Don't spoil my day! Don't mention Mike Sorrell. Anyway, getting back to Jake, he does love me.'

'He told you?'

'Yes, he did.'

'Do you love him, Mag?'

'Yes. Very much.'

'You're very brave, Maggie.'

'Oh, Sam, I'm very lucky . . .'

Samantha Matthews was glad she had insisted that they stay at Brown's Hotel. It was handy to Piccadilly, Bond Street and just about everywhere else, being in the centre of the West End. It was easy to walk to all the shops, and cabs were readily available.

Now as she hurried down Albermarle Street, making her way back to the hotel, she could not help wondering what Maggie had been doing this afternoon. Her friend had insisted on going off alone, and had behaved in the most secretive way. But she would soon know; Maggie would eventually tell her.

It was hot and muggy this afternoon and a storm threatened. Samantha decided to ask the head porter to order a car and driver for the evening ahead. They were going to the theatre and then on to dinner at The Ivy and the last thing they needed was to be caught in the rain.

When she entered the lobby Samantha made straight for the porter's desk. After ordering a car, she took the lift up to the suite she and Maggie were sharing. It was her treat, her birthday present to Maggie. 'But you've already given me that gorgeous bag!' Maggie had protested when she had made the announcement in Scotland. Samantha had merely smiled at the time and refused to listen.

Maggie was still out.

Samantha dropped her bag and packages on the sofa in the sitting room and went through into the bedroom. Taking off her dress and stepping out of her high-heeled shoes, she put on a silk robe and lay down on her bed. She was tired from rushing around all day and wanted to relax before dressing for the evening.

After a moment her thoughts settled on Maggie. She loved her like the sister she had never had, and there was no one she felt closer to, or cared more about. Not unnaturally, given the circumstances, she was worried about Maggie. It was she who had introduced Maggie to Jake Cantrell, and she felt responsible for the current situation. On the other hand, Maggie was a forty-four-year-old woman who was highly intelligent and extremely smart. If she didn't know what she was doing, then Samantha didn't know who did.

Samantha sighed under her breath. There were no doubts in her mind about Maggie's capabilities, and in many ways she admired the attitude she was taking about the baby. But what about Jake? Would he come through for Maggie? And what if he didn't? Could Maggie really manage to bring the baby up on her own? That took guts, which Maggie had, of course. She'll be all right, no matter what, Samantha decided. And I'm there to help her. Samantha smiled to herself. Their motto had always been: through thick and thick and thin and thin.

The telephone on the nightstand between the two beds began to ring. Reaching for it, Samantha said, 'Hello?'

'Is that you, Samantha?'

'Yes, it is. Who's this?' she asked, failing to recognize the somewhat gruff male voice at the other end of the line.

'It's Mike Sorrell, Sam.'

Samantha was so surprised she almost dropped the receiver. 'Oh!' she exclaimed and then added in an icy tone, 'What can I do for you, Mike?'

'I'm looking for Maggie.'

'She's not here.'

'When do you expect her, Sam?'

'I don't know,' Samantha replied, as cold as ever, ignoring his attempt at friendliness.

'Have her call me, please.'

'Where?'

'I'm staying at the Connaught.'

'You're in London!'

'I'm here on business.'

'How did you know where we're staying?'

'I tracked you down, via your assistant in Connecticut. When all I could get was Maggie's answerphone, I phoned your studio.'

'I see. I'll give her the message.'

'Thanks,' he said.

'Goodbye,' Samantha muttered and slammed the phone down. She glared at it. *Son of a bitch*, she thought and angrily zapped on the television set. She got the BBC and the evening news, but watched it somewhat absentmindedly, wondering what Maggie's ex-husband wanted with her.

Half an hour later Maggie walked into the suite laden with shopping bags. 'Hi, Sam,' she said, walking through into the bedroom, putting the packages on a chair and kicking off her shoes. 'It's just started to rain. Perhaps we'd better get a car for tonight.'

'I already did,' Samantha replied and pushed herself into a sitting position on the bed. 'Sit down, Maggie darling. And brace yourself.'

Maggie stared at her. 'Why? What's wrong?' She frowned, then continued, 'There *is* something wrong. I can tell from the dour expression on your face.'

'Guess who's in London? No, you'll never guess. Don't even try. It's Mike Sorrell. He just called you, about half an hour ago. He wants you to phone him. He's staying at the Connaught.'

'Good God!' Maggie flopped into the nearest chair and stared at Samantha, shaking her head in disbelief. 'How did he find us? Not that it's a secret where we are.'

'Through Angela. When he couldn't raise you he called my studio.'

Maggie bit her lip, suddenly thoughtful. 'Out of

the blue he wants to talk to me. I wonder why.'

'As do I, Mag. Are you going to call him?'

'I don't know. What for? It can't be anything to do with Peter or Hannah, he would have told you if there was some sort of problem or emergency.'

'I think he would. He sounded calm enough and controlled.'

Maggie thought for a moment and then made a decision. Pushing herself to her feet, she looked at Samantha and said, 'I'm going to talk to him now, get this out of the way.' She walked into the sitting room looking brisk and businesslike.

Samantha slid off the bed and followed her.

Maggie lifted the phone on the desk, asked the operator to connect her to the Connaught Hotel and a few seconds later she was talking to Mike Sorrell.

'It's Maggie. I hear you want to talk to me.'

'Hi, Maggie! Yes, I do. I was hoping we could get together.'

'Oh. Why?'

'I need to go over something with you. How about tonight? I thought we could meet for a drink. Or dinner.'

'Certainly not.'

'Not even a drink?'

'No. I'm busy this evening.'

'Tomorrow?' he suggested.

'Why can't we talk now, on the phone? That's what we've been doing, off and on, for the last two-and-a-half years.'

'I need to see you in person, Maggie.'

'Are the twins okay?'

'Oh yes, they're fine. Look, I think we have some unfinished business to discuss.'

Startled to hear this, Maggie was silent for a moment. Then she made another decision. 'Nine o'clock tomorrow morning. Here at Brown's Hotel. I'll meet you in the lounge.'

'Okay! Great. 'Bye, honey.'

Maggie put the receiver in its cradle and turned around, stood leaning against the desk, staring at Samantha. 'You're not going to believe it, but that snake in the grass just had the temerity to call me honey.'

'Something's not kosher in the House of Denmark, to paraphrase Hamlet!' Samantha exclaimed indignantly. 'Since you've seen fit to meet with him, I'm glad you made your venue here. I'll be ready and waiting in case you need me . . . to kill that son of a bitch.'

Maggie couldn't help laughing. 'Oh Sam darling, I do love you. No matter what, you can always bring a smile to my face.'

Grinning, Samantha leapt to her feet and went over to the small bar. 'Let's have a vodka on the rocks before we get ready for the theatre.'

'Good idea. You fix it. I want to get something from the bedroom.'

Maggie returned a moment later, carrying a small package. 'This is for you, Sam. It's just to say thank you for all this – ' She glanced around the sitting room. 'But mostly it's because you're always there for me, and always have been.'

Samantha took the package, tore off the wrapping

paper and opened the red velvet box. It contained a pair of delicate chandelier earrings made of gold and malachite.

'Oh Maggie, how sweet of you! The earrings I admired in that shop in the Burlington Arcade. Thank you so much, they're gorgeous. But you shouldn't have.' She went over and hugged Maggie, and added, 'Your friendship is the most important thing in the world to me.'

Maggie drew away from her, and smiled lovingly. 'Through thick and thick and thin and thin . . .'

The following morning when Maggie got up she wondered, for a moment, why she was feeling so tense. Instantly she remembered. Mike Sorrell was coming over to the hotel to see her, and she was not looking forward to it at all.

Very simply, she had nothing to say to him, and she didn't particularly want to hear what he had to say to her. As far as she was concerned they had no unfinished business, as he termed it. Their business was well and truly finished and had been for a very long time.

'You look fantastic!' Samantha exclaimed, when Maggie walked into the sitting room of the suite a few minutes before nine. 'The bloom is on the rose, and then some, Maggie. You look so well and so happy he's going to be gnashing his teeth.'

'I doubt it,' Maggie said, and grinned. 'I'm sure he's very happy with his lady love, his new wife. He's probably in the midst of starting a brand new family. That's what these second, trophy wives want, isn't it?

Kids galore and an insurance policy for the future?'

Samantha laughed. 'Who knows? And who cares? Listen, Mag, I've been thinking about your situation with Jake, and I'm really glad. I know it's going to work out.'

Maggie patted her stomach. 'And the baby?'

'I think you're doing the right thing. Having it, I mean. Just make sure I'm godmother.'

'Who else but you?' Maggie looked at herself in the mirror, straightened the lapels of her navy blue gabardine suit, adjusting the collar of her white silk shirt as she did. 'Give me twenty minutes with him and then come downstairs and get me.'

'I will. Our appointment at Keith Skeel's antiques place is set for ten o'clock anyway.'

'See you in a few minutes,' Maggie murmured and left the suite.

Mike Sorrell was already waiting for her in the lounge when she arrived a few seconds later. He rose to greet her, seemed at a sudden loss, as if he didn't know whether to kiss her or shake her hand. He opted for the latter, and thrust his hand at her.

Maggie shook it quickly and sat down opposite him. She could not help thinking that he looked weary, worn and sad. His face was lined and jowled, his hair very grey, and in general there was a tired air about him. He wasn't wearing well, she decided, and looked much older than forty-nine. An image of Jake, twenty years his junior, flashed before her eyes. She blinked and averted her face, not wanting him to see the sudden smile of pleasure that had settled there. He might misunderstand that smile.

She said, 'Let's order coffee, shall we?'

'Thanks. I could use another cup.' As he spoke he signalled to a waiter. Turning to Maggie he asked, 'Do you want anything to eat?'

She shook her head.

Once he had given the order for coffee, Mike turned back to her, again looking uncertain.

Maggie seized the moment and said, 'Why did you want to see me?'

Mike cleared his throat nervously. 'I was in New York at the end of last week, en route to London for a client. I thought we could get together there. I'm sure Samantha told you I called her studio when I couldn't reach you.'

'Yes, she did. But *why* do you want to see me at all? You dumped me unceremoniously almost three years ago now, and have hardly been in touch since then. Why the unexpected change of heart?'

When he remained totally silent, Maggie added, '*I* don't think we have any unfinished business. Quite the contrary, our business is well and truly finished.' She laughed a little acidly. 'You made that quite clear to me when you left me for your legal colleague.'

'Don't be bitter, Maggie,' he murmured. 'I realize now that –'

'Bitter!' she exclaimed, cutting him off. 'I'm not bitter. I've better things to do with my time than waste it feeling bitter about you, or mourning your loss, Mike. I have a life to live, and believe me I'm living it. To the hilt.'

'You look very well . . . glowing,' he said, eyeing her thoughtfully.

Maggie decided he sounded slightly regretful and wondered what was happening in his new life. But she really didn't care, and she didn't want to know. She said, 'Look, Mike, I have an appointment with an antiques dealer this morning, so my time is limited. What's this unfinished business you mentioned on the phone? Let's get to the point.'

He took a deep breath and said, '*Us*, Maggie. We're the unfinished business. We were together for so long, we had a good life, and we have the kids . . .' His voice trailed off as he became aware of her icy demeanour, the disdainful expression on her face.

Maggie's voice was frosty when she said, 'Are you trying to tell me you made a mistake? Is that it, Mike?'

'Yes, for my sins, I did. I should never have left you, honey. We were the best, so good together. As I said, we had a great life – '

'*You* did,' Maggie interrupted. 'I didn't, now that I look back. You were pretty selfish and self-involved, you never really thought about my needs, and the one time I was happy, doing so well at the design firm, you made me leave my job. You just couldn't stand the fact that I had an interest other than you.'

'Don't be like this, Maggie. *Please*.'

She laughed in his face. 'You bastard! You dump me in the most cold-hearted way, barely talk to me for nearly three years and now come around making nice talk. What's all this about? Don't tell me your new wife's left you?'

When he sat back in his chair and glared at her, Maggie knew she had hit the mark. 'Well, well, well,' she said, biting back an amused smile. 'And more than likely for a younger man. Right?'

Mike Sorrell flushed deeply, but still he said nothing.

Maggie said, 'Ironic reversal.'

'I suppose it is,' Mike agreed at last. 'And yes, Jennifer has left me. She took up with a guy about six months ago, unbeknown to me, of course. Anyway, she's gone off with him. Permanently. To Los Angeles. She wants a divorce.'

'Never mind, Mike, you'll manage to cope somehow. I did.'

'Can't we try again, Maggie?' he pleaded. 'Let's give it a shot. The kids are all for it, too. And I need you.'

'Oh, really? Well, it might surprise you to know that I don't give a damn that you need me. Also, what Peter and Hannah think doesn't concern me very much. They have behaved in the most unconscionable way with me. So, my attitude is exactly the same as theirs has been towards me since you dumped me for a younger woman. Let's not forget what you did.'

'Don't be so resentful and bitter!' Mike exclaimed, glaring at her. 'I'm offering you this chance to start all over again, to put the family back together again, and you're behaving as if I'm asking you to commit suicide or murder.'

'Apt words, very apt words indeed!' Maggie exclaimed. 'To come back to you *would* be suicide. And you murdered my soul for years, all the years I knew you, Mike. You never let me be me, be myself.'

'You don't want to end up a lonely old woman, all

by yourself, do you?' he asked and then paused as the waiter arrived with the coffee.

Once he had left, Maggie said in an icy tone, 'You egotistical idiot. What on earth makes you think I'm alone? As a matter of fact, I'm very involved with someone.'

'Is it serious?' he asked, and he was unable to keep the angry look off his face.

'Yes, very serious. I expect to be married soon.'

'Who is he?'

'I don't think that's any of your business. We're divorced, remember.' Maggie pushed back her chair, stood up and stepped away from the table. Then she paused and murmured, 'Goodbye.'

As she walked through the lounge she saw Samantha hovering in the doorway. She raised her hand in greeting and smiled. She felt freer and happier than she had in years. In a few days she would be back with Jake. Her future.

CHAPTER
11

JAKE HAD TO KEEP reminding himself that the speed limit was forty-five miles an hour, to resist the temptation to press his foot down hard on the pedal. He was on his way to Maggie's, and he couldn't wait to get there.

She had called him on his bleeper the minute she had arrived at her house in Kent from Kennedy Airport, and when he had asked her if he could come over she had agreed at once. He thought she had sounded glad to hear his voice, excited even, and this pleased him. He had missed her; he wondered if she had missed him.

Ten minutes later he was driving into her yard.

Before he had even turned off the ignition she was coming out of the kitchen door and running down the back steps. Her face was wreathed in smiles.

'Hi, sweetheart!' he cried, slamming the truck's door behind him and almost running towards her.

They met in the middle of the back yard, and he swept her into his arms and swung her around. They were both laughing when he finally set her down on the ground.

Jake held her away from him, looking into her face, smiling widely.

Maggie smiled back at him and exclaimed, 'I've missed you so much, Jake! I can't begin to tell you how much!'

'I know, I've missed you too,' he said and brought her into his arms, kissing her deeply on the mouth. Once he started kissing her he couldn't stop. He showered her with kisses. Her forehead, her eyes, her face and her neck. 'I'm happy you're home, Maggie.'

'Yes, so am I. Let's go inside, Jake.' She cocked her head on one side and gave him a flirtatious look. 'I have something for you.'

'You do?' He looked at her questioningly.

She nodded, took hold of his hand and led him into the house. Her suitcases were still in the kitchen, along with her raincoat and a shopping bag; she reached into the latter and pulled out a package.

Turning, she offered it to him, feeling suddenly rather shy and girlish. 'This is for you, Jake. It's from Scotland.'

Grinning, and just a bit flustered, he took the gift from her and stared at it for a moment. 'What is it?' he asked finally.

'Open it and see,' she answered, gazing up at him.

He did so, pulled out a heavy fisherman's sweater made of thick cream wool and then looked at her. 'Maggie, this is great. But you're spoiling me.'

'I just hope it fits. I had to guess your size. Large, right?'

He nodded and then held it against himself. 'I'm sure it's perfect. Thanks, Maggie.' Putting the sweater down on a chair he moved forward, pulled her into his arms and kissed her on the cheek. 'Thanks . . . for thinking of me when you were away . . .'

'I never stopped, Jake.'

The adoration reflected in her eyes told him what he wanted and needed to know. He bent into her, placed his mouth on hers and kissed her passionately.

Maggie held onto him tightly, returning his kisses, matching his ardour, pressing herself against him, needing to feel his warmth and his love.

Finally, he slackened his hold on her and stared down into her face. 'Can we go upstairs?'

Maggie nodded.

Together they climbed the stairs holding hands.

It occurred to Jake that their lovemaking was more frantic and passionate than ever. They shed their clothes and came into each other's arms with a rush of excitement and urgency; they seemed to grasp at each other, their faces full of intensity and longing.

Jake found himself taking her to him at once, on her urging, and she was hot and yielding and ready for him, as he was for her. They soared together, clutching each other tightly, calling each other's name as they rose higher and higher, lost in the wonder of each other.

When he finally fell against her he felt drained, almost exhausted from their passion. 'Oh God, Maggie,' he gasped. 'It's never been like that. Not ever. Not any time. Not anywhere. Not even with you. Until now.' He raised himself onto one elbow and looked down at her. 'That was a first.'

She smiled and touched his face. 'Jake . . .'

'Yes, sweetheart?'

'I love you . . . I love you so much . . . more than I've ever loved anyone.'

'Oh Maggie, Maggie.' He wrapped his arms around her, held her close to him. 'I've wanted to hear you say that for ages. I love you too. But then you know this . . . I told you the first night.'

'I felt the same way, but I just wanted to be sure. About my own feelings, I mean.'

'And are you sure now?'

'*Absolutely*.'

'I'm glad.'

Maggie lay next to him, her arms wrapped around him, drifting with her thoughts. Finally rousing herself, she said, 'Jake, I have a surprise for you.'

'Mmmmmm,' he murmured lazily without moving.

Maggie tried to sit up. He held her tightly in his arms, would not release her. Struggling slightly, she said softly, 'Let me get up, Jake. I have something to tell you.'

'Tell me then.'

'I'd like to be looking at you when I do.'

'Oh.' Intrigued, he let go of her and sat up himself.

Maggie crawled in front of him, then sat curled up in a ball, staring into his face.

'So go on, tell me, sweetheart,' he said, eyeing her curiously.

Maggie smiled. 'I'm pregnant, Jake. I'm expecting a baby. Our baby.'

A beatific smile spread across his face and his eyes lit up. 'That's wonderful! *A baby*. That's great, Maggie! It really is.'

'You *are* pleased then?' she asked.

'Sure I am. I always wanted a child. I told you that. When did you realize? When is it due? I wonder if it's a boy or a girl?' For a few moments he was full of questions.

Maggie answered each one, enjoying his excitement and happiness, relieved that he had reacted in this way.

Later they made love again. 'To celebrate the baby,' Jake whispered in her ear and then they fell asleep in each other's arms.

It was Jake who awakened first, about half an hour later. He slid out of bed and went into the bathroom where he took a shower.

When he returned to the bedroom wrapped in a towel, Maggie was putting on a loose silk caftan. She turned around as he came in; as always she felt the impact of him ... his dark good looks, the soulful green eyes, the black hair slicked back after his shower never failed to surprise her. There were moments when he took her breath away.

'You're staring,' he said.

'I know. Sorry. It's just good to see you that's all.'
For a moment she was tempted to tell him about the
night they first met at the Little Theatre in Kent, when
Samantha had called him Tom Cruise. But she
refrained, knowing that the story would not sit well
with him. He disliked references to his good looks
and his physique.

Maggie moved across the room swiftly, the caftan
flaring out behind her. 'I picked up some groceries
on the way in from the airport. Steaks and salad for
dinner. How does that sound?'

'Great. I'll be down in a minute. If you open a bottle
of wine we can have a drink outside, while I grill the
steaks on the barbecue.'

'It's a deal,' she said and went out.

After he had buttoned his white shirt, pulled on his
blue jeans and boots, Jake went downstairs. He found
Maggie outside on the back terrace, sitting at the table,
the bottle of wine in an ice bucket. She poured two
glasses as he sat down next to her.

'Cheers,' they said together, clinking glasses.

After taking a long swallow, Jake remarked,
'Things are going great at Havers Hill, Maggie. And I
know Mark and Ralph have been giving you progress
reports. But I can't wait for you to come out to the
site tomorrow. You'll be very surprised, pleasantly
surprised.'

She grinned. 'I know I will. I guess I'll have to make
two trips tomorrow. One in the morning and one at
night. I do want to see the outside lighting after dark.
You said some of it was in place already.'

'But only temporarily. For you to see. I've rigged it

up in such a way that if you don't approve we can change it. My guys haven't done the channelling in the ground for the wires. We'll do that once you've made your final decision.'

'I wish you'd been with me in Scotland, Jake. I found some wonderful antiques.'

They sat talking about the work at Havers Hill for a while, and then they went into the kitchen. Maggie made a green salad and put it on a tray, along with plates, knives, forks and napkins. Jake insisted on carrying this outside for her; Maggie followed him with the plate of steaks.

'I've rarely seen fireflies,' Maggie said, clutching Jake's arm. 'Look! Over there! The little lights dancing among the bushes.'

'You're right!' he exclaimed. 'I haven't seen them since I was a kid myself. When I was about fourteen. Amy and I would go to her aunt's –' Jake broke off, sat back in his chair, sipped a little coffee, suddenly silent and tense.

Maggie said, 'Why did you stop?'

'It's not a very interesting story,' he mumbled and got up. He walked along the terrace and stepped down onto the lawn which stretched in front of it.

Aware of the sudden change in his mood, sensing that something was troubling him, Maggie rose and went after him. She caught up with him on the lawn, took hold of his arm and pulled him around to face her.

'What is it, darling?' she asked, filling with apprehension.

He stood staring down at her and shook his head. A deep sigh escaped him. 'I really didn't want to tell you this tonight. Not on your first evening back. I just wanted us to enjoy being together. But I guess I have to tell you . . .' He sighed again, then put his hand on her shoulder, peered into her face. 'I've got some really bad news, Maggie.'

She stared at him. 'What kind of bad news?'

'It's about Amy . . .'

'The divorce has stalled, is that it?'

He shook his head. 'No, not in the way you mean. But it is stalled.'

'You always said she was very reluctant to divorce you, and I can't say I blame her,' Maggie murmured, feeling deflated after the excitement of earlier and their intimate dinner.

'It's not really her,' Jake began, and stopped. He coughed, and said in a low voice, 'While you were away I found out that Amy has cancer. Ovarian cancer.'

'Oh no, Jake, how terrible! I'm so sorry. Is she getting treatment?'

'Chemotherapy. She started at the beginning of this week. Maybe the treatment will arrest the cancer.'

'Let's hope so,' Maggie said, and moving away she trailed across the lawn, knowing what he was going to say before he said it. She knew because she knew him. He was a decent man, and he was sensitive, compassionate.

Jake caught up with her and put his arm around her shoulders. 'I have to help her as much as I can,

do what I can for her, Maggie. You do understand
that, don't you?'

'Yes. Of course.'

'I just can't pressure her about the divorce right
now.'

'I understand . . .' Maggie paused, took a deep
breath and went on quietly, 'Are you moving back to
New Milford? Are you going to live with Amy again?'

'No, I'm not! How could you think that?' he cried
and turned her to face him. 'I love you, Maggie. I
don't want to lose you. I just want you to understand
that I'll have to do what I can for her, especially financially. She's on my medical insurance, I can't pull that
away from her. If we got divorced she'd lose her
benefits. She needs me to be there for her right now.
She's like a child, she's always been dependent on
me. As soon as the cancer's arrested I'll talk to her
again about seeing her lawyer.'

Maggie compressed her lips and nodded. She was
afraid to speak. She didn't want to say the wrong
thing. She didn't want to lose him either. Her eyes
filled with tears.

In the dim evening light he saw them glittering on
her dark lashes, and he brought her into his arms,
pressed her head against his shoulder. 'Don't cry. I
know what you're thinking. You're thinking about
the baby.'

'Yes,' she whispered against his shirt which was
soaked with her tears.

'Will you marry me, Maggie? When we can?'

'I will, Jake. I love you.'

'I love you. I want you and I want our baby. But I

have to stand by Amy. Until she's better. You do understand that?'

Maggie nodded. 'If you weren't the kind of man you are, I don't believe I would love you as much as I do. I'll wait for you, Jake. I'll wait.'

CHAPTER
12

'IT'S ME, AMY,' Jake called out as he opened the door of her apartment. Bending, he picked up the bags of groceries he had deposited on the floor and went into the hall. Walking across the living room, he stood in the doorway. 'Hello, honey,' he said, smiling at her.

Amy was sitting on the sofa in the dim-lit room, watching television. 'Hi, Jake,' she said in a low voice and gave him a wan smile.

'I'll be with you in a minute, Amy. After I put all of this stuff in the kitchen.'

Amy nodded and leaned back against the sofa. She was so happy to see Jake but she didn't seem to have the strength to show it.

Jake thought she looked excessively pale today and

weaker than usual, but he made no reference to her health. Turning, he hurried into the kitchen; after placing the groceries on the table he glanced around. For the past few weeks Mary Ellis, the wife of one of his electricians, had been keeping the apartment clean. She was doing it more as a favour to him and out of the goodness of her heart rather than for the money, and he was pleased with the results. The kitchen was not only neat and clean, it sparkled.

Once he had put everything away, Jake went back to the living room and sat down opposite Amy. 'How're you feeling today?' he asked, inspecting her face closely, thinking she was thinner than ever.

'Tired, Jake, a bit done in,' she answered.

'Do you want me to make you something to eat before I go back to work?'

She shook her head. 'I'm not hungry . . . I'm never hungry these days. But you eat something.'

'No, thanks anyway. I can't stay too long. I have to get back to the site as quickly as possible, we're doing some special wiring. When do you have to go to the hospital again?'

'Tomorrow. My mother's going to take me.'

'What does the doctor say? Are you in remission yet?'

'I think so. But that doesn't mean I'm not going to die, Jake. Not many people survive cancer. We all know that,' she murmured in a low voice.

'You mustn't be negative, Amy,' he replied gently but firmly. 'And you must keep your strength up. Not eating is the worst thing you can do. You need nourishment, some good food in you. Why don't you let me make you something? I did a lot of shopping at the supermarket. I bought all sorts of things, special things you've always liked.'

'I'm not hungry, Jake,' she began and stopped, her voice quavering. Amy took a deep breath, opened her mouth to say something and stopped again. The tears came then, welling in her eyes. Slowly they trickled down her pale cheeks.

Jake got up immediately and went and sat next to her on the sofa. He put his arms around her and held her close. 'Don't cry, Amy. I said I'd look after you, and I will. It's going to be all right, you're going to get better. This is the hard part, you know, undergoing the treatment, suffering through it. I know it's making you weak, but you'll get your strength back eventually. And when you do I'm going to send you and your mother to Florida for that vacation I promised you.'

'You'll come won't you, Jake?' Amy asked, looking at him wistfully.

'You know I can't. I've got to work, I must make sure things keep running smoothly. I can't let anything slip, not now.'

'I wish you *could* come though.'

'I know you do. Listen to me, Amy, you and your mother are going to enjoy getting away. It'll do you both good.'

'Jake . . .'

'Yes, honey?'

'I don't want to die.' She began to cry again, sobbing against his shoulder. 'I'm frightened. I think I'm going to die. I don't want to. I'm afraid, Jake.'

'Hush. Hush. Don't upset yourself like this. Remember what I've said to you before, it's the worst thing you can do, getting yourself so overwrought in this way. You've got to stay calm, be positive. Everything's going to be all right, Amy. Hush now.'

Eventually she stopped weeping, and as soon as she was composed Jake got up and went to the kitchen where he boiled a kettle and made a cup of tea. He brought it to her on a tray and sat talking to her for a while, wanting to allay her worries and fears, hoping to help her reach a better frame of mind.

Jake was preoccupied with thoughts of Amy as he drove to South Kent. He was doing everything he could to help her, but she had to help herself. Her doctor had told him that a positive attitude could work wonders, and that many people had licked cancer because of this. Jake knew only too well how negative Amy was; he wished he could make her understand how important it was for her to look on the bright side, to vow to get better and to do everything she could to achieve this goal. But she was more negative than ever, apathetic, and gloomy. He was doing everything he could, from providing financial support and doing the shopping to coming over whenever he could to sit with her, to cheer her up.

By the time he arrived at Havers Hill Farm Jake had decided to have a talk with Amy's mother. Maybe she could make more of an impression than he had been able to with Amy.

After parking the pick-up, he made directly for the kitchen before going to check up on Kenny and

Larry, who were working on the exterior wiring.

Maggie's briefcase was on the floor and her papers were spread out on the old kitchen table, as they usually were, but she was nowhere in sight. He ran up the stairs and found her in the master bedroom, measuring one of the walls.

Hearing his footsteps, she swung around and her face lit up at the sight of him. 'Good morning!' she cried, coming towards him.

His smile was wide, and he was so intent on sweeping her into his arms he did not notice the frown of concern, the worry lurking at the back of her eyes. She knew how much he was juggling – the business, his own work, Amy's illness, and herself. That he was exhausted was apparent.

Hugging her to him, Jake said, 'How're you feeling, Maggie? How's the baby doing?'

She smiled up into his face, pushing her worry to one side. 'We're both terrific and all the better for seeing you. Were you at Amy's?'

'Yes. I got her some groceries.'

'How is she, Jake?' she asked, her brows puckering in a frown.

He shook his head. 'Not too good. Down. Depressed, I think.'

'Who can blame her? How awful for her to be so ill. She's so young. It's very sad.'

'I just wish she had your kind of spirit, your positive nature, Maggie; that would help a lot, I think.'

Maggie nodded and slid out of his arms. 'Come on, I'd like to show you something.' She was purposely changing the subject, wanting to distract him, to cheer him up, since he seemed to have been infected by Amy's dourness this morning.

Taking him by the hand she led him downstairs and into the dining room. 'Yesterday the table arrived from the antiques dealer in New York. Take a look.' As she spoke she whipped off the dustcloth, and stood back, admiring it yet again.

'What beautiful wood!' Jake exclaimed. 'And it's an old piece, I can see that.'

'Fairly old, nineteenth century. And it's yew.'

Jake glanced around. 'This room's really taking shape,' he remarked and walked over to a wall where Maggie had glued on swatches of fabric and carpet, plus a paint chip. 'Tomato red?' he said, raising a brow eloquently.

Maggie laughed. 'That's right. Heinz tomato soup with a dash of cream. Avocado-green carpet . . . that's as far as I've got with possible colours.'

He laughed with her, much to her relief. At least she had managed to take his mind off Amy's illness for a moment or two.

Jake said, 'I've noticed something lately. Whenever you speak about colours you do so in terms of food.'

'I'm pregnant remember. I've got all sorts of cravings.'

'You don't have to remind me, I could never forget.' He leaned into her, kissed her on the cheek. 'I'm going outside to see the guys. How about supper tonight? I'll feed you.'

'You're on,' she answered, grinning at him.

CHAPTER
13

'ARE YOU LISTENING TO ME, AMY?' her mother said, quickly glancing at her daughter out of the corner of her eye, not wishing to take her eyes off the road ahead.

'Yes, Mom, I am. You said Jake thinks I'm too negative about my cancer.'

'That's correct,' Jane Lang murmured. 'He says it would be better for you if you got out more, *did* things when you're well enough, when you're not in pain. Are you in pain now, Amy?'

'No, Mom, I'm not. I don't know what he means by *do* things. We didn't do much when we were married. He was always working, working, working, a real workaholic that guy is for sure.'

'What do you mean *were* married. You're still

167

married to him, Amy, and let's not forget that. If you would only concentrate on Jake I'm sure you and he could get back together. He loves you, honey, and I know you love him. It was ridiculous of you to split up. He's so nice, I've always liked him since you were kids.'

'I don't think he wants to come back, Mom.'

'But just consider the way he's looking after you right now, Amy, taking care of you financially, doing so many things, like getting you this woman to help you in the apartment, and paying for it. And going to the supermarket for you. He loves you, I'm certain.'

'Oh, I don't know, maybe he's just being nice. He's like that.'

'Like what, honey?'

'*Nice*, Mom. Jake's always been kind to me, ever since we were kids in high school,' Amy responded, sounding slightly impatient.

'You never did tell me exactly *why* you and Jake broke up, *why* you decided to get a divorce. What was the reason?' Mrs Lang asked.

'I don't really know, to be truthful, Mom. I guess we just sort of drifted apart, you know . . .' Amy's voice trailed off. She wasn't really sure how the whole mess *had* come about.

'You can win him *back*! It will give you a goal . . . you must try very hard, Amy, put all your heart and soul into it. You and Jake were always right for each other, it's such a shame all this came to pass.' Mrs Lang sighed and then applied pressure to the brake as she turned a difficult corner on the slippery road. 'And it's such a shame you didn't have children.

I don't know why you never planned a family. Amy –'

'It's a good thing I didn't!' Amy exclaimed, cutting her mother off, 'now that I'm dying. Where would they have been? Practically orphans with their mother dead of cancer at the age of twenty-nine and their father working night and day, never home.'

'Don't talk like that, Amy, it's very upsetting to me. And you're *not* dying. Dr Stansfield told me you're doing well.'

'He did?'

'Certainly he did.'

'When, Mom?'

'This afternoon. When you were getting dressed. He thinks you're making wonderful progress.'

'I don't feel that I am,' Amy mumbled. 'I'm not really in pain but I feel crummy, Mom. Really crummy. I told Aunt Violet that when I was in the kitchen tonight, you know, when she was cooking the hamburgers. She offered me a vodka, said it would make me feel better.'

'That woman is incorrigible at times!' Mrs Lang exclaimed.

'She's your sister, Mom.'

'And we're as different as chalk and cheese.'

'I guess so.'

'I know so. Anyway, honey, we're going to take that trip to Florida next month. You'll enjoy it very much. Jake mentioned it to me again this morning when he called. Do you remember when your Daddy took us to Florida? You were six. You loved it so much.'

'Perhaps I'll get to see Mickey Mouse before I die,' Amy murmured.

'Don't, Amy, *don't*,' her mother whispered.

'Sorry, Mom. But I do hope I get to meet Mickey.'

'You will, you will, when we go to Disney World,' Mrs Lang said, peering ahead. Although it was a wet night the rain had stopped; knowing Amy was tired, wanting to get her home, Mrs Lang pulled out, impatient with the slow-moving Toyota in front of her.

She did not see the vehicle coming directly at her down the other lane on the two-lane road. Blinded by glaring headlights, Jane Lang took one hand off the wheel to shade her eyes and in so doing relinquished a degree of control of her car. But she didn't have a chance. The oncoming truck, moving at an even greater speed, smashed into them head on.

Amy heard her mother screaming and the sound of glass shattering. She felt the impact most forcibly, was thrown forward and then back like a helpless rag doll.

'Mom,' she said before she blacked out.

Amy was suddenly and inexplicably outside the car, floating above it in the air, just in front of the windscreen. She could see her mother inside, pinioned by the steering wheel against the front seat. And she was there, too, sitting next to her mother in the other seat. At least her body was there. Amy realized that she and her mother were both unconscious in the car.

Below her, there were other people milling around now. The driver of the truck which had struck their car, who was himself unscathed; other drivers whose cars were backed up behind because of the crash. Then she heard the sound of sirens and saw two state troopers arriving on their motorbikes.

I'm dying, Amy thought; no, I'm actually dead. I've already died and left my body. She could see that body. She was floating over herself, looking down at the empty shell.

Amy was not afraid. Nor did it matter to her that she was dead. In fact, she felt extremely happy, free of all pain and sadness, and without a care in the world.

Unexpectedly, Amy was being sucked forward as if by a giant vacuum hose. She was in that hose. It was not a hose, she discovered, but a long tunnel. She was being pulled up it by some great force. But she still felt good, not in the least upset, even though she was dead.

At the very end of the long tunnel she could see a tiny pinpoint of light. As she continued on her way, rushing towards the light, it grew bigger and bigger, and so much brighter. Soon she emerged from the tunnel, blinking, adjusting her eyes to the light. It was the most magnificent light. She was surrounded by it, enveloped in its warmth and brilliance. The light embraced her, made her feel lighthearted, and so happy. She had never experienced feelings like this ever in her life before. They were feelings of tranquillity and peace and unconditional love, and they came from the all-embracing light. She basked in it.

Amy was floating in the light, totally weightless; she had shed her cumbersome human body. And she realized she had entered another world, a different dimension, and that she was pure spirit.

Soon she became aware of other spirits, floating in the brilliant light. They were sending her love and warmth and they did so without speaking. But somehow they were communicating. She reciprocated their love, beaming it to them, and she knew they welcomed it.

The light changed, its white brilliance picking up prisms of colour, all of them rainbow hues. Another spirit drew closer to her, accompanied her, and Amy understood that she was being guided now, gently wafted towards a destination by this spirit. She knew without being told that this spirit was an old soul, that her name was Marika. It was Marika who was moving her along, but tenderly so, and with great love.

The light was growing softer and softer, losing its sharpness. Amy was moving out of it and into the most beautiful landscape she had ever seen. It was a place without a blemish, perfection, paradise. And it was a place without pain, one that was filled with purity and goodness.

The landscape where Amy floated was one composed of green pastures, flower-filled glades, wooded hillsides above a shimmering blue lake. Surrounding this pastoral setting were mountains capped with glittering white snow, and everything was bathed in golden sunlight.

Floating over the glades were many spirits like herself. Somehow Amy knew that there were old spirits mingling with younger souls. And then she saw him.

Her father. The sight of him took her breath away. She knew it was him. Even though he was in spirit form, pure essence, as she was, Amy felt that special love flowing from him to her, and it was the self-same love she remembered from her childhood.

At this moment she felt her mother's spirit floating towards her father. Her mother's aura was radiant and serene, not the crushed human body which Amy had left behind the wheel of the wrecked car. Her parents joined each other and came over to her. They spoke to her. Although no actual words were used, she understood everything. They told her how much they loved her. They said they were waiting for her, but that she must go back for a while. *It is not time*, her mother was saying to her. *It was my time, Amy, but not yours. Not yet.* Their great love for her was enveloping her, and she was not afraid; she was happy.

Marika, the old soul guiding her, explained that she must move on. Soon they were floating through the bright light once more, entering a crystal cave that shimmered and radiated an intense and most powerful light.

Amy was immediately aware that she was in the presence of two women, that they were ancient spirits of great wisdom, and that some of their wisdom was going to be imparted to her. She was told by Marika that she would understand it all, understand the universe, the meaning of everything.

The cave was beyond imagining, made entirely of crystal rock formations and giant stalactites which glittered in the white light, sent out hundreds of thousands of prisms of coloured light, ranging from pale yellow to pink and blue.

Amy was momentarily blinded by the clarity of light in the crystal cave, and she blinked several times.

A moment later she saw more clearly than she had ever seen before. She saw her past life, saw herself, and she understood at once why she had failed in her earthly life. It was because of her negative approach, her apathy; and she was made to understand that she had wasted much, had thrown away the special gifts she had been given. The two women spirits explained this, and Amy felt contrite and sorry.

Then she saw Jake. She saw him at this very moment in time, as if he were right here with her. But he was not. He was in a room somewhere, and he was with a woman, a woman he cared about. A woman he loved. Deeply loved. She recognized the fulfilment and warmth between them. Instantly Amy understood his life. She saw him in the past, in the present, in the future. His whole life was there for her to view, as if she were seeing it on film.

Now Marika was conveying something, saying that she must leave, must move on, but Amy did not want to go. She fought going. She wanted to stay here. Suddenly she was spinning out of the cave, pushed along by Marika.

Marika was urging her in a gentle way to go back to the tunnel. She did not want to and she fought it. She yearned to stay here in this paradise where there was only peace and happiness and unconditional love. But Marika would not permit it. She said she must return.

Amy was hurtling down the tunnel, moving through the darkness, leaving that shimmering dimension behind, leaving the light.

She felt a sudden push and there she was back on an earthly plane, floating again above her mother's wrecked car with their bodies trapped within.

Amy saw the truck-driver and the other drivers and state troopers still hovering near the car. And then an ambulance slowed to a stop. She continued to watch as her mother was removed from the car, and then her own body was lifted out and put on a stretcher.

With a sudden, awful jolt Amy went back into her body.

Eventually she opened her eyes. And then she closed them again. She felt so tired, so exhausted. There was a pain in her head, a terrible pain as if someone had been hammering on her forehead. She fell into unconsciousness immediately.

Amy's aunt, Violet Parkinson and her daughter Mavis rarely, if ever, left Amy's side at the New Milford Hospital. Jake had to come and go because he had to attend to his business, had to work, but he was genuinely concerned about her, apprehensive about her reaction when she finally regained consciousness to learn that her mother had been killed in the terrible car crash.

Jake was also worried about Amy's own injuries. She was badly cut and bruised, and whilst the doctors believed she had no internal injuries, she *was* in a coma.

Now, on the third evening after the accident, Jake sat by the bed in the hospital, holding Amy's hand. They were alone for the time being. He had sent Mavis and Aunt Violet downstairs to have coffee and sandwiches, since they had apparently been sitting with Amy throughout the day.

His thoughts drifted for a while. He worked out some complicated wiring systems for Havers Hill in his head, and thought for a moment or two about Maggie, and then he looked up, startled, when Amy said: 'I'm thirsty.'

Immediately bringing his attention to her, he exclaimed, 'Amy, honey! Thank God! You're awake!'

'I've been in another place, Jake,' she began in a whispery voice. 'I want to tell you about it.'

He nodded. 'I'll say you have, Amy. Unconscious for three days. Did you say you were thirsty? Let me get you some water.'

'Jake!'

'Yes, Amy?'

'My mother's dead.'

He was so startled he gaped at her, and for a moment he was unable to say a word.

'Don't tell me she isn't, trying to protect me, because I know she's dead.'

Jake, who had stood up, now bent closer to her, gave her a puzzled look. 'Let me go and fetch the water, and tell the doctor you've regained consciousness, honey.'

'I died too, Jake, but I came back. That's how I know my mother's dead. I saw her spirit with my father's spirit.'

Sitting down on the chair again, he asked gently, 'Where, Amy?'

'In Paradise, Jake. It's such a beautiful place. Full of light. A place you'd like, you've always been fascinated by light.'

Jake was speechless. He simply sat there holding her hand, not knowing what to say, truly startled by her words.

Amy sighed lightly. 'My mother's safe there. And she's happy now. She's with my father. She always missed him, you know.'

'Yes,' he answered, still at a loss. He wondered whether it was the drugs talking. Certainly the doctors had given her a number of injections, although he was not sure what these were. She was so calm, so in control, and this was mind-boggling to him. He had known Amy most of his life, and he would never have expected her to act like this after her mother's death. They had always been close, and why Amy wasn't hysterical he would never know. Yes, perhaps it was the drugs talking when she had said, a moment ago, that she had just died herself but had come back.

As if reading his mind, Amy remarked quietly, 'I did die, Jake. Believe me.'

He stared at her, a small frown knotting his brow.

Amy sighed. 'I'm tired. I want to go to sleep.'

'I'll get the doctor, Amy.' He extracted his hand from hers, and rose, moved to the door. 'I'll bring the nurse so that she can give you a drink of water.'

'Thanks, Jake.'

He nodded and left the room.

*   *   *

'It was the weirdest thing, Maggie,' Jake said quietly, looking across at her intently. 'When Amy finally came out of her coma tonight she told me her mother was dead. She wasn't hysterical like I thought she would be, but calm. In control.'

Jake shook his head, took a swallow of his beer. 'She also said something else that was strange.' He hesitated.

'What was that?' Maggie asked.

'She said her mother was with her father. In another place. A place she'd been to . . . she called it Paradise. I thought about her words all the way here from the hospital. How did Amy *know* her mother had died in the crash, Maggie? She's been unconscious since it happened.' He exhaled. 'That's what mystifies me.'

Maggie sat back in her chair and regarded him for a long moment, then she said, 'Maybe Amy knew her mother had died because she did see her in another place, just as she claims.'

'I'm not following you,' he answered, giving her an odd look.

'It's possible that Amy had an NDE.'

'What's an NDE?' Jake asked, lifting a brow.

'Near-Death Experience. There's been a lot written about them in the last few years. Doctor Elisabeth Kubler-Ross, the social scientist, who used to practise in Chicago, wrote an article on the terminally ill during her tenure at Billings Hospital at the University of Chicago. This eventually became the basis for her book, *On Death and Dying*, which I found fascinating. She wrote a number of other books, and appears to believe in Near-Death Experiences. As do many people actually, Jake. And doctors as well. Doctor Raymond Moody did the first anecdotal study of the phenomenon. Another expert is Doctor Melvin Morse who has also written several books about Near-Death Experiences.'

'So you're saying that Amy told me the truth?'

'Very possibly . . . most probably, actually.'

'How do you explain an NDE, Maggie?'

'I don't know, I don't think I can . . . because I don't really know enough, Jake,' Maggie murmured. 'There are a few good books available, as I just mentioned. Perhaps you should read one.' Leaning forward slightly, pinning him with her eyes, Maggie went on, 'Did Amy describe this place she went to?'

'No. She just said it was very beautiful.'

'Did she mention anything about light?'

'Well, yes, she did. How did you know that?'

'Because light, very bright light, always figures in Near-Death Experiences. People feel as if they are embraced by the light. Some even think they are transformed by it.'

'Amy did say it was a place I'd like because it was full of light.'

'Anything else?'

'No, I don't think so.'

'And when exactly did she tell you this?'

'The moment she woke up – when she first came out of the coma.'

'Then perhaps she did have a Near-Death Experience. She certainly didn't have enough time to invent such a thing, invent that kind of story. Anyway, deep unconsciousness, or coma, is supposed to wipe the slate clean, wipe the mind clean,' Maggie pointed out.

'Okay, so let's say Amy did have an NDE, what exactly does that mean? To her?'

'It's an experience that she's not likely to forget, for one thing. Apparently people who have them never do, the experience stays with them always, for the rest of their lives. Of course they are as baffled by them as everyone else, and they generally look for meanings, special meanings behind them. An NDE does make people change . . . that brush with death and a glimpse of the afterlife does have an effect.'

'You seem to know a lot about Near-Death Experiences, Maggie,' Jake murmured, eyeing her speculatively.

'Well, I haven't had one myself, but I have talked with several people who have. I did quite a lot of charity work when I lived in Chicago, and I worked at a hospice for terminally ill people several afternoons a week for over four years. That's when I first heard about NDEs. People recounted their experiences to me, and the thing is, they drew such enormous comfort from them.'

'So you do believe there is such a thing then?'

'I guess so, Jake. I don't *disbelieve*. I'm not that arrogant. One would be a fool to dismiss these things out of hand. How can anyone debunk Near-Death Experiences? Or life after death? Or even the idea of reincarnation, for instance? None of us knows anything. Not really. There are far too many unexplained things in this world. I'd be the last person to say that the paranormal doesn't exist. Or couldn't happen. I've got an open mind.'

'Amy doesn't read a lot,' Jake volunteered. 'So I'm sure she doesn't know anything at all about Near-Death Experiences from books, Maggie.'

She nodded. 'There has been quite a lot on television about them, over the past few years, but I'm quite positive Amy did have some sort of experience. I don't think she's inventing this, not for one moment.'

'Why do you say that?'

'From what you've told me about her, Jake, Amy doesn't have the imagination to invent such a thing.'

'You're correct there,' he agreed. Jake leaned back in the chair, stifling a yawn.

Maggie exclaimed, 'Oh Jake, you're so tired after your vigil at the hospital. I think you'd better go to bed. You need your rest, you've got to be up so early tomorrow. We've got the meeting at the farm.'

He nodded. 'I am pretty bushed. But thank God we've finally finished the last design plans for the farm. Lately they seem to have been endless.'

She laughed. 'Only too true. But isn't Havers Hill now looking perfectly wonderful?'

'It sure is, thanks to you, Maggie of mine.'

IT WAS A GOLDEN, shimmering October day. The foliage had already changed, and the trees were a mass of copper and gold, russet and pink, brilliant in the bright sunshine.

Amy feasted her eyes on the landscape at the back of Jake's little house on Route 341, thinking how magnificent everything looked. Such breathtaking colours, such fire in the trees. And the sky was a perfect blue, without a single cloud. It was a mild day, mild enough for her to sit here without a jacket, which she had shed earlier when she and Jake were having lunch.

She rested her head against the chair and closed her eyes, enjoying the warmth of the sun on her face. She felt relaxed, at peace.

Earlier in the week Jake had asked her what he could do to make her feel better, and she had said she wanted to have a picnic out in the country. It had been his idea to bring her here to his new house, and she was glad he had. It was nice to see where he lived, now that they were no longer together. Also, she liked his yard with its beautiful trees, pretty garden and the pastures beyond. He had even shown her around his studio-workshop in the red barn, which had pleased her.

Hearing his footsteps on the path, Amy opened her eyes and sat up.

Jake said, 'Here we are, honey. Ice cream and apple pie, just as you requested.'

Amy smiled at him. 'You're spoiling me. And I'm enjoying every minute of it.'

He placed the tray on her lap. 'Tea or coffee later?'

'Tea, please, and thanks for this.' She glanced down at the ice cream. 'Oh Jake, you remembered how much I love pistachio and raspberry mixed together.'

Jake nodded and grinned, pleased that she was happy. She never complained, but he knew she was frequently in pain these days. If bringing her here and having a picnic with her helped to alleviate her suffering then he was all for it.

'Be back in a minute, honey,' he said, and strode down the path to the kitchen. 'And don't wait for me. I'm only having coffee.'

Amy ate some of the ice cream, enjoying it, but she couldn't finish it all. Her appetite was poor, and she was only able to take a few bites of the apple pie.

She leaned back in the chair again, waiting for Jake to return to the garden.

Strains of music suddenly filled the air and she smiled to herself, knowing that he had somehow managed to wire the garden and put speakers outside. Kiri Te Kanawa singing 'Vissi d'arte' filled the air, her magnificent voice soaring into the sky.

'Where's the music coming from, Jake?' Amy asked when he was back, standing over her, offering her the cup of tea.

'The singing rocks, just over there in the flower beds,' he explained.

She laughed in delight and he laughed also. Then he said, 'Don't you want any more dessert, Amy?'

'No, thanks, Jake, but what I ate was delicious.'

He took the plate away, and then sat down next to her with his mug of coffee. 'I hope you've enjoyed the picnic, being out in the country,' he murmured, glancing at her.

'I have, and it was nice of you to give up your one free day. I know how precious Sundays are to you.'

'I've enjoyed it too, Amy. You know I'll do anything to help, to make you feel better.'

Turning slightly in the chair, Amy focused her eyes on him. She loved him very much. He was the only man she had ever loved . . . since she was twelve years old. He had always been so special to her; he had made *her* feel special. And he had been so kind. Always. Amy had considered herself the luckiest of women to have him, to be his wife; her friends had envied her. But she knew they were focusing on his good looks. Only she really knew what a truly nice person he was.

Jake said, 'You're staring at me, Amy. What's wrong? Do I have dirt on my face?'

She shook her head. 'I was just thinking how long we've known each other.' She paused, cleared her throat and then went on carefully, 'Mavis took me to see the lawyer on Friday, Jake, and I –'

'But Amy, you don't have to worry about the divorce right now. Just get yourself better first.'

'I didn't go to see him about the divorce. A divorce is not necessary.'

He sat looking at her, his expression unchanging. He was not sure how to answer her.

She said, 'I'm dying, Jake. I'm not going to see the end of the year . . . I know that.'

'But Amy, the doctor said you were making good progress!' he cut in swiftly.

Amy shook her head. 'He might think so, but *I* know I'm not. Anyway, I went to see the lawyer because I wanted to make a will. It's necessary now that my mother's dead. She left me her house in New Milford, you know, and her furniture and everything else she owned. And a little money. So, I made a will and I've left everything to you.'

Jake stared at her speechlessly. Then he said, 'But what about Aunt Violet and Mavis? They're your next of kin.'

'No, they're not. You are, Jake Cantrell. You're my husband. We're still married, even though we might not be living together. And as your wife I am leaving you all my worldly possessions. Except for a few items for Aunt Violet and Mavis, you know – some bits of my mother's jewellery, china, that kind of thing. I want you to have everything else.'

'I don't know what to say,' he began and stopped abruptly, staring at her.

Amy gave him a small smile. 'You don't have to say anything, Jake.'

'If that's the way you want it, then thank you, Amy,' he murmured, not knowing what else he could say.

'There's something I want to say ... I want to apologize to you, Jake, tell you how sorry I am that I was a bad wife.'

'Amy, for God's sake, you weren't a bad wife!' he cried. 'You did the best you could, always. I know that.'

'My best wasn't good enough. Not for you, Jake. I was always so negative and apathetic, and I never helped you when you were trying to make a better life for us. I did everything wrong, and I'm truly sorry.'

He stared at her silently, again at a loss for words.

Amy said, 'I really did die the night of the crash. I did leave my body. My soul did, I mean. Or my spirit, if you prefer to call it that. I went to another plane, to another dimension. And I saw my father. Then my mother joined him, and that's how I knew she was dead. There was an old soul there looking after me, and she took me into a crystal cave of wisdom. There were two wise women spirits, and they told me things. And they showed me how wrong I'd been. I saw my whole life, Jake; I saw my past and I saw your past.'

Jake was silent.

Amy said, 'I can't change anything in my life now because I have no time to do so. I have become the person I should have always been, and I must try to make amends.' Amy leaned back in the chair and focused her eyes on Jake. 'You're sceptical, aren't you? I mean about my dying and coming back.'

'No, as a matter of fact, I'm not,' he replied. 'I do know there are other people who have had similar experiences, and a number of books have been written about them.'

'I didn't know that, although I didn't think it could have happened only to me.'

'What happened to you is called a Near-Death Experience, Amy.'

Amy nodded then closed her eyes. After a moment she opened them. Leaning forward, she fixed them on Jake.

He blinked. They seemed brighter, more full of life than he'd ever seen them, and the smile spreading itself across her face was one of pure radiance.

Amy said, 'I not only saw my past, and your past, Jake. I also saw your future. I didn't see mine because I don't have one. Not on this plane at least.'

'You saw my future,' he repeated.

'Yes, I did. There's a woman in your life, Jake, and you love her very much. She is older than you, but that is of no consequence. You and she are meant to be together. You were always meant to be together, and your whole life has been a journey towards her. As hers has been a journey towards you. Once you were souls who were joined together as one, and then you were split asunder. Your whole lives have been spent trying to get back to each other. When you found each other you became whole. Never doubt her in any way.'

Jake opened his mouth but no words came out.

She said, 'This woman, your soulmate, is carrying your child. She's five months pregnant. The baby is due in February. It's a boy, Jake, you're going to have the son you always wanted. The future is good for you. You will be prosperous; you were always right to start your own business. It will go well, and this woman, who is devoted to you and will be your wife, will also be your partner in your business. You are going to have all the things you always wanted, Jake, and somehow never managed to get with me. But you must not let your success change you, or turn your head. You're such a good person. You must cling to your values always.'

'Amy, I don't know what to say. It's true, I did meet someone. In April. I never mentioned her to you because I didn't want to hurt your feelings –'

'Don't say any more; it's not necessary. I am the one who hurt you. This was shown to me, and I was sent back in order to put things right with you and to help you with your future.'

'Help me how?'

'To show you the way, to set you on the right path. You have already started out on it with your soulmate. She is strong, wise, and you must always listen to her.' Amy nodded. 'You must take her advice. And you must also follow all of your instincts. You are usually right. Trust yourself more.'

'I don't know what to say,' Jake began and stopped.

Amy was looking at him intently and he realized how lovely she was. It seemed to him that at this moment she had undergone a startling transformation. Her face was radiant, her pale blue eyes bright and sparkling, and even the curly blonde wig she was wearing looked suddenly right on her.

'Now it's my turn to say you're staring at me,' Amy exclaimed.

'I was thinking how beautiful you looked.'

'I am. *Inside*. I want you to promise me something, Jake.'

'Yes, Amy, I will. Tell me what it is.'

'I want you to promise me you'll get married immediately after I die. I don't want you to have any mourning period. That would be false anyway, since we've been separated for almost two years.' She paused and gave him a very direct look. 'Longer, if you think of the years we lived together without communicating. Do you promise?'

Jake nodded.

Amy went on, 'I think I'll die soon, Jake.'

'Oh Amy . . .'

'There's something else I need to say to you and it's this: love is the most important thing in the whole world.'

'I know you're right,' Jake responded.

Amy smiled her radiant smile and said softly, 'I'm not afraid to die. Not anymore, Jake. You see, I know there is life after death. Not life as we know it here, but life on another plane. I will be glad to shed my body, then my spirit will be free at last . . .'

CHAPTER
15

MAGGIE STOOD STARING out of the kitchen window, wondering what had happened to Jake. It was snowing hard, the tiny crystalline flakes sticking to the panes. She always worried about him in bad weather. The roads could be so treacherous.

Christmas traffic, she decided, that's what was holding him up. He had promised to be here by two, but perhaps he had been delayed at the Little Theatre in Kent. At Samantha's request he had gone up there to look at one of the lighting systems which had blown the night before. None of the stagehands knew how to fix it permanently. Since Jake had designed it, Samantha and Maggie knew he would be able to solve the problem.

Maggie's thoughts drifted to the play for a moment.

The Crucible had opened in September and, much to everyone's surprise and delight, it was still running. It was a sell-out at weekends; Samantha was in her element as the producer, director and owner of the theatre.

Turning away from the window, Maggie walked across the room, her steps slower these days. She was seven months into her pregnancy. The baby, a boy, was due in two months and she couldn't wait to deliver. The baby was big and she was heavy; and every day she seemed to grow slower and slower.

Sitting down at the kitchen table, she looked at her list of gifts. She had finished almost all of her Christmas shopping, having started it earlier in the year. Today was Saturday the sixteenth of December, and anything else she still needed Jake would have to buy. Maggie knew she did not have enough energy to struggle through the stores, the big stores at any rate.

At least she wouldn't have to do much cooking. She and Jake were going to spend Christmas Day with Samantha. That was the big day, of course; on Christmas Eve Samantha was coming to them along with some of the cast and other members of the theatrical group. Weeks ago Maggie had decided to make the supper a cold buffet, so much simpler for her to handle.

Rising, Maggie lumbered into the small sitting room and walked over to the tree. Jake and she had decorated it slowly, gradually, over the past two weeks, mostly because he was so busy with business. And she was unwieldy, not very much help to him.

Maggie smiled inwardly and put her hands on her stomach. The baby was her treasure. Hers and Jake's. He couldn't wait for the child to be born, and was forever pampering her, treating her like a piece of crystal.

Stepping up to the tree, she eyed it critically, knowing that certain branches were still rather bare. Perhaps today they would have time to stop at The Silo to buy some more gold and silver icicles, gold angels and fruits. She and Jake had created a gold and silver tree, with touches of red and blue here and there; and it was eyecatching, she thought.

Maggie walked slowly back to the kitchen and stood at the window again, waiting for him, wishing he would get home. After a while, she moved away, went to the radio and turned it on.

'Hark! the herald-angels sing, Glory to the new born king. Peace on earth and mercy mild . . .' a female voice was singing on the Christmas record the station was playing.

Maggie was immediately distracted. She heard the pick-up coming into the yard and stood looking at the door expectantly, waiting for him.

As always, she felt the impact of him in the pit of her stomach whenever she saw him, even after a very short absence. What it was to be so in love. Sometimes she worried that she loved him far too much.

'Hi, sweetheart,' Jake said, striding over to her, tracking snow across her clean floor.

But Maggie did not care. 'Hello, darling,' she answered, beaming at him. 'I was beginning to worry, wonder what was taking so long.'

'That stupid system I invented!' he exclaimed, brought her into his arms and kissed her cheek.

'Oh Jake, your face is cold, and your hands. Why didn't you put on your gloves and a scarf?'

He grinned at her boyishly. 'Oh stop worrying about me. I'm fine. Anyway, the system's okay for tonight and tomorrow. But I think I'll have to rig up something else next week. Samantha's going to kill me if I don't get it perfect, and this one's not.'

'Do you want a cup of coffee?'

Jake shook his head. 'I think we'd better get going. It's snowing hard, and the snow's settling. It's going to take us a good half hour to New Milford. Do you have the plant for Amy?'

'It's over there on the counter top.'

Jake walked over and looked at it. 'You've made it look pretty with the blue and silver bow, Maggie.'

She nodded. 'Shall we go, Jake?'

'Yes. Let me get your coat.'

The snow had stopped falling by the time they arrived in New Milford, and the sun was shining in the brilliantly blue sky.

Maggie held onto Jake's arm tightly as they walked down the path. There was a light covering of snow on the paving stones, and she was afraid she might slip.

'Here we are,' Jake said a few seconds later. 'Now, just let me undo this.' As he spoke he pulled the wrapping paper off the plant and shoved it in his pocket. Bending down, he placed the miniature evergreen on the new grave.

Straightening, he turned to Maggie and put his arm around her. 'I'm glad we came,' he murmured. 'I gave her my word we would. "Come and visit my grave as soon as you can after you're married," she said and then she made me promise.'

'She's at peace now,' Maggie said. 'Out of her pain and suffering.'

Jake nodded. 'Her soul is free. She wasn't a bit afraid to die in the end.'

Maggie pulled off her gloves. Leaning over the grave, she straightened the blue and silver bow. Her broad gold wedding ring gleamed brightly in the afternoon sunlight. 'That's because Amy knew where she was going,' Maggie murmured.

Jake merely nodded and put his arm around his wife protectively. Together they stood in silence at the grave for a few moments, lost in their own thoughts. Jake was thinking of Amy, who had died ten days ago. He had known her most of his life, and she had been his high-school sweetheart. Somehow everything had gone awry with them. Still, in the end, they had remained friends. He was glad of that, and happy that he had been able to give her comfort in the end, had helped her through her illness. He had been with her when she died, and her last words had been for him. 'Bless you, Jake,' she had said. 'And your soulmate and the baby.'

A week after her death he and Maggie had married, fulfilling Amy's wish that they do so immediately. He had wanted it that way himself, and he knew that Maggie had too. The wedding had been at Samantha's house in Washington; Sam had insisted. She had also arranged for a local judge, who was a friend of her family, to perform the short ceremony. She and Alice Ferrier, the costume designer from the drama group, had been the witnesses.

Jake knew he would never forget last Saturday morning. Their wedding day. Maggie had looked so beautiful and full of life. She had worn a blue wool maternity dress that reflected the colour of her eyes but did little to conceal the fact that she was seven months pregnant. Neither of them cared. Maggie's eyes had been full of tears when the judge pronounced them husband and wife, as his had been. They had both been very emotional that morning, and for days afterwards.

Sam had given a small lunch and members of the cast of *The Crucible* had come in to toast them and wish them well before going off to the Little Theatre in Kent. It had been the most special day of his life.

Jake said, 'I think we'd better go, Maggie. It's starting to snow again.'

Together the two of them walked along the path that led to the gate of the cemetery. At one moment Maggie glanced up at the sky, and high above them she saw the arc of a rainbow. It was indistinct but it was there. She blinked in the bright sunlight and looked away. When she turned her eyes to the sky again the rainbow had disappeared.

She held Jake's arm as they continued on down the path, and at one moment she said quietly, 'The cycle of life is endless, and it never changes.'

'What do you mean?' he asked, glancing down at her, frowning.

'There has been a death . . . and soon there will be a birth. That's the way it is. *Always*. One soul has gone to her rest, a new soul is about to be born in a few months.'

Jake nodded and was silent as they made their way out of the cemetery and back to the Jeep. Once he had helped Maggie in and settled himself in the driver's seat, he leaned in to her and kissed her cheek. 'I love you, Maggie of mine,' he said. Looking at her huge stomach he placed his hand on it and added, 'And I love our baby. He's going to be born well blessed.'

'Oh I know that,' Maggie said, smiling into his eyes. 'Come on, darling, it's time to go home.'

Home, Jake thought, as he put the key in the ignition and turned it. *Home.*

Her Own Rules

Barbara Taylor Bradford

Meredith Stratton, at forty-four the owner of six elegant international inns, is about to celebrate her daughter's engagement. At this seemingly happy time in her life she begins to suffer from a strange illness that baffles everyone. Her doctor cannot find a physical cause for her debilitating symptoms, and, desperate for answers, she seeks the help of a psychiatrist. Through therapy Meredith peels back the layers of her life to discover the truth behind her most careful creation – herself.

Determined to get well, Meredith traces her roots back to another country where she learns about childhood experiences that dramatically changed her life. What she discovers is not only the key to the past but to her future happiness and fulfilment as a woman.

Barbara Taylor Bradford's new novel addresses the universal themes of love and loss, passages and renewals, and the inexplicable twists of fate that shape our lives.

ISBN 0 00 224152 8

Dangerous to Know

Barbara Taylor Bradford

Sebastian, the fifty-six-year-old patriarch of the Locke clan, is handsome, charismatic, a man of immense charm and intelligence. He heads up the philanthropic Locke Foundation, funded by the vast family fortune built by his forefathers. Committed to relieving the suffering of those in genuine need, Locke travels the globe, personally giving away millions a year to the poor, the sick, and the victims of natural disasters and wars. He is seen as a beacon of light in today's darkly violent world. That is why the police are so baffled when Sebastian is found dead in mysterious circumstances. Has he been murdered, and if so who would want to kill the world's greatest philanthropist? Could such an upstanding man have enemies?

Vivienne Trent, an American journalist, met Locke as a child, married him, divorced him, but stayed close to him. Aware that there was another side to this enigmatic man, she sets out to find the truth about his death and about Locke himself.

'Few novelists are as consummate as Barbara Taylor Bradford at keeping the reader turning the page. She is one of the world's best at spinning yarns.' *Guardian*

ISBN: 0 586 21739 8

Everything to Gain

Barbara Taylor Bradford

Mallory Keswick is a woman with the world at her feet. Then out of the blue, that world is shattered by violent tragedy and she loses all that she holds dear.

Torn by grief, Mal knows that she must rebuild her life. She flees to a village on the Yorkshire moors where she learns to draw on the deepest reserves of her spirit, and to look life in the eye once more.

Returning to Connecticut, Mal opens a café and shop selling gourmet food and kitchenware and turns it into a highly successful venture. But there remains in her life an aching void, a grief that no individual, nor her new-found business acumen, can assuage. Then she meets Richard Markson, and once more, Mal's life has come to a crossroads. It is he who shows her that she has everything to gain – but only if she has the courage to take it.

Totally absorbing and heartrendingly real, *Everything to Gain* lays bare Mallory's life to expose powerful feelings that are startlingly familiar, because they are our own.

'Heart-rending stuff ... *Everything to Gain* is truly uplifting'   *Today*

ISBN: 0 586 21740 1

A Woman of Substance
Barbara Taylor Bradford

In 1905 a young kitchen maid leaves Fairley Hall. Emma Harte is sixteen, single and pregnant.

By 1968 she is one of the richest women in the world, ruler of a business empire stretching from Yorkshire to the glittering cities of America and the rugged vastness of Australia.

But what is the price she has paid?

A magnificent dynastic saga, *A Woman of Substance* is as impossible to put down as it is to forget. This multi-million copy bestseller is truly a novel of our times.

'An extravagant, absorbing novel of love, courage, ambition, war, death and passion'   *New York Times*

'A spellbinding family saga . . . A *tour de force*'   *Annabel*

'A rags-to-riches blockbuster . . . brilliantly told'
Manchester Evening News

ISBN 0 586 20831 3

Hold the Dream
Barbara Taylor Bradford

Emma Harte was the heroine of Barbara Taylor Bradford's multi-million copy bestseller, *A Woman of Substance*.

Now she is eighty years old and ready to hand over the reins of the vast business empire she has created.

To her favourite grandchild, Paula McGill Fairley, Emma bequeaths her mighty retailing empire with these heartfelt words: 'I charge you to hold my dream.'

A towering international success and the glorious sequel to *A Woman of Substance*, this is the powerfully moving tale of one woman's determination to 'hold the dream' which was entrusted to her – and in so doing find the happiness and passion which is her legacy.

'The storyteller of substance'   *The Times*

'A must for all Barbara Taylor Bradford fans'   *Woman*

'I enjoyed every word'   *Daily Express*

'The novel every woman is going to take on holiday'
                                                    Daily Mail

ISBN 0 586 05849 4

To Be the Best
Barbara Taylor Bradford

The enthralling sequel to Barbara Taylor Bradford's universally loved novels, *A Woman of Substance* and *Hold the Dream*.

Set in Yorkshire, Australia, Hong Kong and America, this remarkable contemporary novel continues the story of an unorthodox and endlessly fascinating family. As the spirit of Emma Harte lives on in her granddaughter, Paula O'Neill, an engrossing drama is played out in the glamorous arena of the wealthy and privileged, underscored by a cut-throat world of jealousy and treachery.

Paula must act with daring and courage to preserve her formidable grandmother's glittering empire from unscrupulous enemies – so that Emma's precious dream lives on for the next generation . . .

'A compulsive read'   *Daily Mail*

'Will keep you up till all hours, reading just one more chapter before you can bear to turn out the bedside light'   *Prima*

ISBN 0 586 07034 6